Hostages to Fortune

Also by Joan Lingard

Hostages to Fortune

JOAN LINGARD

THOMAS NELSON INC., PUBLISHERS
Nashville   New York

Copyright © 1977 by Joan Lingard

All rights reserved under International and Pan-American Conventions. Published by Thomas Nelson Inc., Publishers, Nashville, Tennessee. Manufactured in the United States of America.

First U.S. edition

Library of Congress Cataloging in Publication Data
Lingard, Joan.
    Hostages to fortune.
    SUMMARY: When the death of Kevin's employer confronts him and his wife Sadie with the sudden loss of both job and home, an uncertain future looms up before them. Sequel to "A Proper Place."
    [1. Family life—Fiction. 2. Country life—Fiction] I. Title.
PZ7.L6626H04 [Fic]   76-49646
ISBN 0-8407-6539-8/PZ7.L6626H04   [Fic]   76-49646

FOR MARTIN

with love

Hostages to Fortune

Chapter One

MR ELLERSLEY died early one hot July morning. Kevin McCoy heard the news when he went to work. He was cowman on Mr Ellersley's farm.

As he came into the byre, Mr Maxton the farm manager was hastening across the yard. He called out to Kevin, who stopped.

"The boss has died," said Mr Maxton. He sounded hoarse and looked distraught. He was panting slightly, and a few beads of sweat stood on his forehead.

Kevin could not take it in. He frowned. "What do you mean like?"

"He died this morning. Mr Ellersley. Four o'clock it was. A heart attack, so they say. It was all over in minutes."

The two men went into the byre together. The cows were lowing, heavy with milk. They looked up expectantly at Kevin as he passed. The men stood a moment talking about Mr Ellersley, scratching their heads; they were dazed. Then Mr Maxton left Kevin to his work and went out across the farm.

Kevin set to work. Mr Ellersley was dead but the cows were still here, needing to be milked. This was his job; he would get on with it. But even as he did, the thought came to him: would he keep this job now, and all that went with it? Watching the milk flow, his mind returned to Mr Ellersley. He had been a fine man: Kevin had liked him a lot and could not believe he was dead. It was only yesterday that he had seen him. He had come across the yard and stopped to speak to Kevin for a minute or two, asking about Kevin's young brother Gerald who used to work here in the racing stable but now had gone back to Ireland. Kevin had told Mr Ellersley that Gerald seemed to be doing well. Mr Ellersley had said that was good news, that Gerald was an excellent stable-boy and could handle horses beautifully. Gerald had gone through a wild period but seemed to have settled. At least Kevin hoped so, but could not worry about him any more.

So Kevin, heavy-hearted, continued with his work during that warm July morning, as the flies buzzed thickly around the byre, and over the fields the insects hummed. And in the big house, Mr Ellersley lay dead.

Sadie McCoy, Kevin's wife, heard the news when she went to work at the big house. She helped out there in the mornings, with the domestic chores. She took her baby Brendan with her in his pram, parking it outside the kitchen door. That morning she decided that he might as well sit outside, since the weather was so good and he was getting a lovely tan on him. His skin was fairly dark, like his father's, as were his eyes. His hair too was as black as Kevin's but, at the moment anyway, curled all over his head.

"Now be a good boyo, Brendan my love," said Sadie, shaking her finger at him, making him laugh. He could be a right devil at times, kept her on the hop, seldom let her have a minute's peace.

He gurgled, clapping his fat hands together as if she had said something funny.

She opened the back door and went into the kitchen to find Mrs Willis the housekeeper and Mrs Jones the cook sitting at the scrubbed wood table drinking tea. Their eyes were red as if they had been crying.

"Whatever's the matter?" cried Sadie.

"It's Mr Ellersley," said Mrs Willis. "He's dead."

"*Dead*? He can't be. I saw him yesterday, he was sitting in the library writing letters. I spoke to him."

But they told her that he had died early that morning. Sadie sat down beside them, Mrs Jones poured her a cup of tea putting in three spoonfuls of sugar since sugar was considered good for shock.

"I can't believe it," said Sadie.

She too had liked Mr Ellersley, they all had. He had been very kind to them when they had first come, had helped Gerald and had always had time to exchange a few words. They had had many laughs together when she had been dusting the library. She sat with her elbows on the table sipping the sweet tea, trying to remember if he had not looked well. She supposed that he had been a bit tired and grey this past while, and one morning he had been leaning on his elbows looking very weary indeed. But when she had asked him if he was all right, he had said that of course he was, he just needed a holiday. They were to have gone on a cruise to the Canary Islands in August, he and Mrs Ellersley.

And now he was dead.

"I still can't take it in," said Sadie, shaking her head.

The house, and the estate consisting of a racing stable and farm, belonged to Mr Ellersley. There was no son and heir for them to pass to, no children at all from his marriage. There was only Mrs Ellersley, and no one could imagine her running a farm and stable.

"How is Mrs Ellersley?" asked Sadie.

Mrs Willis shrugged. "She never says much, does she? She's locked herself away in the bedroom. I knocked and asked her if she'd like a cup of tea, but she said, 'No thank you', that was all."

Mrs Ellersley was not liked in the way that Mr Ellersley had been: she seldom talked to the staff, except to say what she wanted to be done or not done in the house. In the beginning she had had an aversion to Brendan coming with Sadie, having never liked children much, and when he cried it had got on her nerves. Her nerves were often jangling: they could see it in her face. She was a strange, lonely woman who floated up and down the corridors, never smiling, doing what? They were never sure, apart from changing her clothes which she did several times a day and making up her face from all the dozens of little pots and bottles that she kept on her dressing table. She went to the hairdresser's too, every week, to have her dense black hair reblackened and sculpted. There was never a strand to be seen out of place.

They sat and thought of Mrs Ellersley, not being able to begin to imagine what would happen to her.

"Don't suppose she'll stay on here all alone," said Mrs Jones.
"It's a big place for one woman."

It had been a big place even for one woman and one man but
they had entertained a lot, especially at weekends, when parties
would come and stay from Friday night till Monday morning.

The women, stunned by the death of the master of the house, sat
in the kitchen most of the morning, drinking tea and talking. The
men on the farm worked, and talked little.

Around midday, Mrs Ellersley appeared in the kitchen. Mrs
Jones jumped up and seized a pot. Sadie got down under the table
to pick something up. Mrs Ellersley did not hold much with idle-
ness.

"I wanted to have a word with you about lunch, Mrs Jones," she
said, speaking in her usual voice. But her white face looked even
whiter than normal and the eyes seemed to be staring out of it, yet
at the same time had an air of not really seeing anything.

"Yes, madam," said Mrs Jones. "Is there anything special you
would be fancying today?"

"My brother will be arriving shortly," said Mrs Ellersley. "And
the lawyer."

Sadie escaped up the stairs with her duster, not that she saw
much point in dusting today. Poor Mr Ellersley would not care
whether or not there were a few specks of dust lying on the beautiful antique furniture or along the tops of his gilt-edged pictures.
She trod slowly along the landing, not wanting to pass his door,
which she saw, as she approached, was firmly closed.

"Poor Mr Ellersley," she said softly to herself. "I wish you
hadn't died."

When she went home at lunch-time she found Kevin already
there, sitting by the kitchen table in his shirt sleeves, with the back
door open. They were not very hungry that day, what with the
heat and the sad news. They talked about Mr Ellersley, remembering his kindness, and lamenting his death.

All morning Kevin had been thinking that this could mean a
change in their lives, but did not say so to Sadie, not wanting to
alarm her and give her something else to grieve over. Mr Maxton

said that he thought it was probable that Mrs Ellersley would sell the estate. And if she did there was no guarantee that whoever bought it would employ the present staff, although Mr Maxton, who had been there for more than twenty years, would presumably have a good chance of staying on himself. Anyone taking over would be foolish to get rid of him when he knew the place inside out, but Kevin had only held his job for a few months and the new owner might even want to bring a cowman from his old farm.

Kevin drank a mug of tea after lunch sitting on the back doorstep, looking out over the fields, thinking how he would hate to have to leave this place. It had been their first proper home since they had married, and they loved the peaceful countryside and sweet clean air. Before this, they had lived in Liverpool and London, but it was here that Kevin wanted to bring up his son.

Brendan was lying on a rug in the garden kicking his heels in the air. He was rolling on his back and catching his toes between his fingers and rocking and gurgling. He was a fine healthy baby full of bounce and energy. He had a better chance in life than babies of his age in the North of Ireland where his mother and father had come from; here there was no threat hanging over his head of being bombed or having his house set on fire or of losing his mother and father. Well, perhaps no threat was not exactly true, considering the bombings there had been in England, but certainly less, much less. Gazing out over the quiet meadow, which seemed almost to shimmer in the heat, Kevin wondered at people wanting to kill one another. Why couldn't they enjoy the world?

Sadie came from the kitchen and knelt down behind him putting her arms round his neck. He caught her hands between his and she kissed the top of his head. They were so happy that it seemed a terrible shame that such a good man as Mr Ellersley had had to die. They had not expected it, not at all, for he had not been old, only fifty-five or so. But they needed no telling that life was unpredictable. Their lives had always been.

"Kevin, you don't think—? You don't think we'll have to leave here?" Sadie felt selfish even to be thinking of themselves when Mr Ellersley was lying newly dead.

"Don't know, love. We'll have to wait and see, won't we? Don't worry about it, I expect the new owner will keep us on."

"The new owner?"

"Mrs Ellersley is almost bound to sell. I mean, she couldn't take the place on herself now, could she?"

Sadie supposed not. What if the place was bought by some horrible man whom neither of them liked or wanted to work for? They had been so lucky with Mr Ellersley, they had told one another that many times over, and counted their blessings.

"Oh, Kevin!" A tear dropped on to the top of Kevin's head.

"Now then, Sadie, don't get worked up or the boy won't like it. You have to think of Brendan."

Sadie glanced over the top of Kevin's head at Brendan who had got himself tied in knots but was still laughing and enjoying himself. He seemed to laugh most of the day, and if he wasn't laughing he was shouting, usually with vigour, demanding attention. She and Kevin had come a long way and overcome many things and she knew that whatever happened, they would survive. Given any chance at all. But one always needed a bit of a chance. She tightened her grip round Kevin's neck. He laughed and said she might strangle him. She ruffled his dark hair with her hand, then edged round him down the step and ran across the garden to lift Brendan. She swung him up in her arms, out into a big wide arc, making him laugh with delight. He was not aware that anyone had died, that his life might be in danger of being changed again. As long as he had Sadie and Kevin and their dog Tamsin, Brendan had nothing to worry about.

That night Kevin had a dream. He dreamt that a man in a long black coat, wearing a tall black hat was evicting them from their cottage. "Out!" he was crying. "Out, out, out!" He kept pointing his finger down the path towards the road. Kevin woke, sweating, and muttering, "Out! Out!"

"What are you raving about?" asked Sadie, turning over, pulling the sheet with her, uncovering him.

"Nothing," he said.

He lay awake for the rest of the night.

The funeral took place two days later. Kevin went, Sadie did not, taking Brendan instead for a long walk in his pram through the country lanes. Tamsin trotted alongside them, nose down, tail up, most of the way. The day was full of sunshine; the trees were heavy with the weight of glossy green leaves; birds sang lustily from high branches. Everything in the countryside seemed to be bursting with life. Since Mr Ellersley had died Sadie had been thinking a great deal about life, how marvellous it was, how full of richness and interest. She supposed that she had always known that she enjoyed it, but usually didn't stop to think about it. That was probably the best way but at times it did no harm to remind yourself that it wouldn't go on for ever and you might as well make the best of it whilst you had it.

For a few days everything continued much as usual. Kevin went to work in the byre, Sadie to work in the big house. Mrs Ellersley's brother took her away for a few days and so there seemed even less point doing much in the way of cleaning. Mrs Willis and Mrs Jones pondered gloomily on their future, hating the idea of change.

"But you might not have to leave," said Sadie.

Why did they have to look on the gloomy side? She had decided that she was not going to, she was going to keep her fingers crossed that the new owner would be an absolutely splendid man, who would take an immediate liking to them all, and beg them to stay. At increased wages.

"It would be just like it if you talked him into it," said Kevin with a grin. "Once you start on someone they don't have much of a chance."

"I certainly don't believe in giving up easily."

July continued, full of warm, balmy days, but towards the end of the month the weather changed, becoming cooler, bringing rain for the first time for some weeks. They needed rain on the farm so when Kevin got up one morning and saw it falling he was thankful. He told Sadie, who was lying in bed moaning, that she should think of the beasts and crops; she had had her fill of sun lately.

Mr Maxton came to seek Kevin out in the byre that morning. He looked glum: he had news.

"The place is sold. Yesterday, I believe."

"Sold? Do you know who to?"

"A Mr Allan. Doesn't mean anything much to me."

It meant more that afternoon when Mr Allan arrived to look the place over. He was a portly, middle-aged man from Manchester. He was a property developer.

"A property developer?" said Sadie. "Does that mean he can build houses all over the estate?"

"I shouldn't think so," said Kevin uneasily. "I wouldn't imagine he'd get planning permission for that."

But no one on the farm liked the news at all. It hung over them like a grey threatening cloud. Mr Allan marched busily all over the land, chewing on the end of a fat cigar, nodding at those he passed but saying nothing. He did not look much like a farmer, nor had he known one end of a horse from another, said Bobby, the racing trainer, although he had stood at the door of the stables looking pleased at the sight of the horses, asking plenty of questions there, about which horse had raced where and won what, and how much money they had got. It was a good racing stable, and Mr Ellersley had always done well.

Another day or two passed, during which time the rain came down and everyone waited and wondered. Mrs Ellersley came back but she could not be expected to tell them anything. She gave her orders to Mrs Willis and Mrs Jones, nodded good-morning at Sadie when she saw her busy with her duster along the landing; and in the bedroom Sadie saw signs that Mrs Ellersley was beginning to pack up her things. She even asked Sadie to help her. Whilst they were working together, folding the beautiful clothes, the silk dresses and cashmere jumpers, Sadie longed to speak to the woman, to say something comforting to her, or even just to ask her where she was going and what she was going to do. She could normally speak to anyone, but Mrs Ellersley was too much even for her. Once or twice she did open her mouth and try to start, then stopped, for there was something in Mrs Ellersley's vacant eyes that said, 'Don't speak, don't disturb me, I don't want to be disturbed'.

The bags were packed, the wardrobe empty, the dressing table cleared of its bottles.

Sadie hesitated. "I was really fond of Mr Ellersley," she said.

"I know," said Mrs Ellersley abruptly. "If you'd like any of the things I've left in the drawers just help yourself."

Sadie thanked her. There were many fine things still left in the drawers, including three cashmere sweaters, beautifully soft and in lovely colours, creamy yellow, sludgy green, and hyacinth blue. Sadie rubbed them against her face. Whenever she wore them she would think of Mr Ellersley. Yes, more of him, than of Mrs Ellersley, even though the sweaters had been hers.

Mrs Ellersley was collected by her brother in his long, expensive car and borne off. The lawyer came and said that Mr Ellersley had left seven hundred and fifty pounds each to Mr Maxton and Mrs Willis, and five hundred pounds to Mrs Jones. There had been nothing for Kevin because he had come to work here after Mr Ellersley had made the will, but, said the lawyer, Mrs Ellersley herself wished to give Kevin one hundred pounds. She had said that she knew her husband would have wanted Kevin to have something. When Sadie heard she was overcome with remorse and wished she had tried harder to speak to her, for, after all, she must have liked them to give them the money. And now she was perhaps hundreds of miles away, and Sadie might never see her again. She would not be able to thank her, not properly; she could get her address from the lawyer and write her a little note. 'Dear Mrs Ellersley, Thank you very much for the hundred pounds. It was very kind of you.' How could that begin to tell what Sadie felt?

"Now then," the lawyer went on, taking off his spectacles to look at the assembled company of workmen from the estate, "I have something further to tell you."

Not one person in the room liked what he heard. Mr Allan was keeping on the racing stable and a small part of the farm, but the rest of the property was going to be covered with houses. Planning permission had not come through fully yet but was expected to at any moment, since the pressure for land for houses was great in this area. Everywhere in Cheshire, as in other parts of England, estates of new houses had mushroomed in the last twenty years. This particular corner was not to escape any longer.

"So the stable stays," said the lawyer, "and everyone who works there. Also the house staff, Mrs Willis and Mrs Jones." He turned to Mr Maxton. "I'm pleased to be able to tell you, Mr Maxton, that your services will also be retained, to manage the small farm that will be left. But it will be small, and the dairying side is to be axed."

At that, Kevin's heart plummeted like a stone to the bottom of a pool. Somehow, he had known this was coming, had felt threatened as soon as he laid eyes on the little fat business man strutting around the land puffing his cigar. He had sensed that his time here was running out. Last in, first out. It was the way things went. The trouble was that they were always last in.

People like them kept getting moved on. They seemed to have no foothold anywhere, no place that they could claim to be their own. He took his handkerchief from his pocket and passed it over his damp forehead. Again, they were to be homeless.

They would have to find a new home, but more than that they would have to find a way to change their lives, to reduce the chance of getting moved on. They would have to get a foothold, even a toehold. But how, and where?

"I'm extremely sorry, Mr McCoy," said the lawyer. He stopped, for there was nothing more that he could say or do: it was not a matter over which he had any control. He was only there to inform them of the contents of Mr Ellersley's will and of Mr Allan's intentions for the future. And that future did not include the McCoys at Ellersley Hall.

"I don't want to go," wailed Sadie when Kevin came home. "I'm happy here. I won't go! Can't we squat or something?"

Kevin said nothing. His face was dark, his eyes brooding. When things were difficult he went quiet, whilst Sadie raged and stormed.

The next morning, the letter came. Mr Allan's agent informed them, with regret, that he must give them notice to leave at the end of August. This gave them five weeks in which to find a new job for Kevin and a new home.

Chapter Two

FOR a moment, after Kevin had read the letter, Sadie was tempted to blurt out her secret. She was going to have another baby. She had meant to tell Kevin the day that Mr Ellersley died but then it had seemed the wrong time, and afterwards Kevin had been so worried and withdrawn that she had not been able to get round to it. She had wanted to wait until things were settled.

She walked to the bottom of the garden and leant on the fence, looking out across the fields. After a difficult beginning she had come to love this place, to enjoy watching the black and white cows grazing, the flowers push up in the spring, the birds flutter around the trees at the back of the cottage. Never before in her life had she had a chance to know the countryside. In her mind she had foreseen them living here for years, Brendan going to the little school in the village, and then the new baby too.

The new baby. She had wanted to have it born here, if not in the house, at least somewhere nearby. Mrs Willis and Mrs Jones would have helped look after Brendan in the day-time until Kevin came back from work. And then when she brought the baby home they would all have settled down again in their cottage to await the spring. For the baby was due to be born at the end of January.

But where would it be born now? The very question panicked

her. Not to know where your child would be born seemed a terrible idea. Even when she had been expecting Brendan they had had two ghastly rooms in Liverpool, but at least they had had them. Now, again, they would have nothing. Nothing! It wasn't fair, it wasn't! She beat her fist against the fence.

Kevin came up behind her and put his hands on her shoulders. "Don't fret too much, Sadie love. We'll find something. Sure haven't we always in the past?"

"But I thought all that *was* past. That's the trouble, having to start again. Just when we'd got settled in and made friends."

"I might easily get a job nearby. Let's go and find the *Cheshire Observer* and see if there are any jobs going."

Kevin spread the newspaper out on the table open at 'Situations Vacant'. It was a familiar thing to be doing this; they remembered full well too many times before. Their difficulty was that they needed a job with a house. There seemed to be a number going without; these they could not look at.

"Here's something," said Kevin, and read out the advertisement. A farmer was wanting general help, on a farm about twenty miles away. Kevin would have preferred something in dairying but right now he could not be too fussy.

"I wonder what the place is like," said Sadie. "It's a pity we haven't bought our wee car yet, we could have taken a run over." They had been saving hard to buy a car and now, with this present of one hundred pounds from Mrs Ellersley, they would be able to get something half decent.

Next day when Sadie was in the village shop she told her friend Pauline, who served there, about the job.

"Twenty miles away wouldn't be so bad," said Pauline. "George and I could come over any time to see you in the car." George was her boyfriend.

"You must promise to come and visit us."

"Hey, why don't I get George to run us all over there this evening? You could take a look at the place and see if you fancy it."

"What a great idea! There's no use Kevin applying for a job if we don't like the place, is there?"

George was agreeable, and with Pauline, picked them up in his little black and white Mini in the early evening. Sadie, Brendan cuddled against her, settled back to enjoy the ride. Now it was beginning to feel less like a disaster and more of an adventure. Oh not that she wouldn't have given everything they had to have stayed where they were, but then Mr Allan wouldn't have been interested in everything *they* had.

George drove at a fair speed, clipping the corners, sometimes alarming Sadie who clutched Brendan tightly. Before she had him she would not have minded how fast anyone drove; now she would rather travel slowly, and safely.

George drew up in front of a gate.

"Do you think we should get out?" asked Sadie.

Kevin thought that they had better not, it might not look too good to be poking around. They wound down the car windows and looked at the house. It was a white-washed house trimmed with black, not anything like as big as Ellersley Hall. It was obviously a different kind of farm, one where the farmer himself would manage it and, as Kevin said, get his boots muddy.

"The barns look O.K.," murmured Kevin.

"The barns!" said Sadie. "Trust you to think of them."

"Sure, don't I spend most of my day in them?"

Sadie was more interested to see where the farm cottages were. George drove slowly along the road, and about half a mile along, they came upon a row of white-washed cottages. Rambler roses grew all over them, in profusions of red, yellow and pink. The gardens in front and behind had been well tended and bloomed with flowers and vegetables. The cottages were one-storeyed, unlike their own which had two rooms up and two down.

"How lovely!" cried Sadie, falling in love with them straightaway.

They were more picturesque than the cottages where they lived now. They had what Pauline called 'old world charm', which made Kevin laugh.

"Pauline's right," said Sadie. "They do have it. I think they're absolutely sweet. You'll need to watch your head going through the door, Kev." He was a good six feet in height and the doors looked low.

He grinned, shaking his head at her. She was already moving in in her head, sitting in the garden smelling the roses, playing with Brendan and Tamsin. She was always ready to jump like a grass-hopper; he himself moved more slowly. But he had to admit the place did look rather good, both the farm itself, and the cottages. Yes, and the cottages.

When they got home Pauline and George roared off, Sadie and Kevin went inside to write a letter. They remembered when Kevin had written his letter for this job; he had done it with their friends Kitty and Bill in Manchester. But this time he wrote with more confidence: he had had several months' experience and also, he knew that Mr Maxton would give him a very good reference.

Mr Maxton wrote the reference next day. It sounded rather formal and stilted, not saying anything very much in particular except that Kevin was a good cowman and a reliable worker. It was not Mr Maxton's way to be effusive. If it had been Mr Ellersley who had been writing it, it would have sounded more impressive.

"He might have sung your praises a bit more loudly," said Sadie.

There was nothing wrong with what Mr Maxton had said, Kevin told her, and farmers didn't expect the kind of things that Sadie herself would write. If it was left to her she would have said so many fancy things that no one would ever have wanted to take Kevin on.

Kevin put Mr Maxton's letter in beside his own, sealed the en-velope and took it to the village to post. With them also went Brendan in his pram and Tamsin. Before returning home they called at the local pub to see the landlord and his wife, Mr and Mrs Hughes. Tamsin was the daughter of their bitch Megan.

"Come away into the kitchen, Sadie," said Mrs Hughes. "And bring the lad with you. Oh yes, and you too, Tamsin! My, isn't Brendan growing? I do believe he gets bigger every day."

He would soon be one year old. It seemed hard to believe and yet, on the other hand, Sadie could hardly remember what it felt like not having him.

She went with Mrs Hughes and told her about the new job and how pleased they felt to have come upon such a nice place so easily.

"That sounds really grand, Sadie," said Mrs Hughes. "I hope you'll be lucky."

Sadie thought that they would be. There had been something about the place that made her feel it would be theirs.

As they walked home through the darkening summer evening she was happy again for the first time since Mr Ellersley had died.

"Let's have a party for Brendan's birthday, Kev."

"I might have known you'd be cooking something else up. You always are, aren't you? You're a real devil when it comes to laying plans."

Sadie tucked her hand into Kevin's arm. He was pushing the pram in which Brendan now lay fast asleep, his chubby hands closed tight above his head. As they walked Sadie talked about her proposed party. She was going to ask Maria to come from Liverpool, and Mrs Hignett, and maybe Mr and Mrs Fiske would bring them down in their van. And she hoped that Kitty and Bill would come from Manchester.

"Wouldn't that be great? To see everybody again."

"'Deed it would." Not that Kevin missed the old neighbours in Liverpool as much as Sadie did; he needed people less. "I'm thinking the party is more for you than for Brendan."

Sadie laughed.

The next day she wrote to them all, telling them they *had* to come!

The following morning, she met the mail van at the gate. "Anything for us?" There would have just been time for the farmer to reply. The postman held out only one letter and she saw at once that it was postmarked 'Tyrone'. She carried it into Kevin.

"Letter from your mother."

Kevin took it from her, she went into the kitchen to wash the breakfast dishes. She hated watching Kevin read letters from his mother: his face always looked dark and troubled. He was the eldest of the nine children in the McCoy family, and since his father had been killed by a bomb in a pub blast two or three years back, he still felt responsible for his family and a bit guilty that he had left them. Every letter that came from his mother contained bad news. She never seemed to think of writing to say they were all doing fine. She moaned and groaned on page after page and tried Sadie's temper sorely. She had sympathy for the woman, but what did she expect Kevin to do for her? Whenever they could they sent money and last year when she had sent the second son Gerald over to them they had looked after him and helped put him on his feet.

Sadie sloshed the dishwater around noisily. She hoped that Mrs McCoy would not be writing for more money. They had little to spare and had a removal to pay for now as well. And there were always extra expenses when you moved into a new place.

Kevin came into the kitchen with the letter in his hand. He was frowning.

"What's up now?" asked Sadie, unable to keep her mouth closed.

"My mother's worried about Clodagh."

Sadie groaned. "Sure she's always worried about something, for dear sake!"

"Wouldn't you be if you'd a tribe of kids like that to look after?"

"I wouldn't be so daft as to have them in the first place."

Kevin glared at her and went out. She sighed. She hadn't meant to say that, having said it many times before, and it never helped. The McCoys were Catholics and believed in large families, at least the older ones had, not Kevin so much. His sister Brede though, who was the same age as Sadie, seemed to believe in having lots of babies too, for she was expecting her third child. But then, thought Sadie, maybe I shouldn't be talking, for here am I about to have another and Brendan not quite one year old yet.

She finished the dishes, went back into the sitting room where Kevin was getting ready to go off to work.

"Sorry! Didn't mean to let fly. What's the matter with Clodagh anyway?"

Kevin shrugged. "Oh, she just seems to be a bit wild, that's all."

"All your brothers and sisters seem a bit wild if you ask me."

But she spoke softly, and not aggressively.

"Some of them aren't, but then Ma doesn't write about those ones. Brede was never wild after all. And Michael's doing rightly on the farm.

"You were wild in your day. Remember?"

He grinned. "You're a one to talk, Sadie Jackson!" He came to kiss her before he left for work.

Quickly Sadie tidied the rest of the house, changed Brendan's nappy and put him in his push-chair. Then she set off up to the big house.

She sang as she dusted that day. They still did the same things in the house even though no one was living in it. Mr Allan had bought the contents along with the property itself. He had said that he wanted everything to be cared for, nothing should be let to go even for a day.

Going into the library today, remembering Mr Ellersley, she thought how strange it was that the death of one man had affected so many people. But she supposed that, in fact, the death of most men did affect many people, when you came to think about it. Take Kevin's father for example. No, she did not want to, not this morning. Kevin's family always seemed to be hovering in the background as some kind of vague threat to her. She fully expected that one of these days a taxi would draw up at the gate and out would come Mrs McCoy and the rest of the children. If she were to fling herself on to Kevin for care and protection he would not turn her away. Sadie let that vision slide away from her. She dusted the books, the desk and the leather chair on which Mr Ellersley had sat.

Next morning, she was at the gate again.

"Anything for us?" she asked, as the postman drew up.

He handed her a buff coloured envelope. A bill.

"Are you sure there's nothing else?" She felt like rifling his bag.

"That's it, Sadie."

She went dejectedly back into the house. Kevin said she was silly, she could not expect a reply to come so quickly from the farmer, it would take a day or two. She was too impatient and would have to learn that other people didn't jump as if a gun had been fired the way she did.

"O.K., O.K." She grinned at Kevin, sticking out her tongue. "But sure aren't we waiting for one of the most important bits of news of our life?"

That Kevin could not deny. And so another day passed, with Sadie making plans in her head, and crossing her fingers every time she thought that things might go astray.

The third morning the postman passed by.

The fourth morning the postman passed by.

The fifth morning the postman stopped.

Sadie rushed out to meet him. She had forced herself not to stand at the gate waiting for him, for it was too disappointing when the van sailed past and all she got was a wave. He opened his bag and brought out three letters. One of them must be it!

She danced back up the garden path into the kitchen where Kevin sat eating his breakfast. She turned the envelopes over.

"Here's one from Liverpool. That looks like Maria's writing. And this is from Manchester."

"That'll be Kitty," said Kevin.

"Who else could it be?" snapped Sadie, who had just turned over the third letter and seen yet another Liverpool postmark. Mr Fiske's writing. "There's nothing from the farmer, Kevin."

"We don't have to give up hope yet, you know, Sadie."

Kevin reached for his jacket and put it on. It was cooler this morning, with rain bringing a little chill into the wind. He went off to work, Sadie sat down at the table and read her three letters. They could all come! That was something. She was thrilled at the idea of having them here, all together.

But her pleasure was dimmed by the fact that Kevin had had no word of the job yet. He must get a letter soon, he must. Couldn't he ring the farmer? she suggested at tea-time. But no, Kevin did not think so; you couldn't go pestering people like that. If they wanted you they would get in touch with you.

Sadie brooded over this as she bathed Brendan for bed. If it was up to her she would be along there knocking at the farmer's door. You didn't get much in this life without pushing for it.

The next morning, the postman's van passed by. And the next. "I guess that's it," said Kevin heavily. "He can't be interested."

Chapter Three

"MAYBE you should have enclosed a stamped, addressed envelope?" said Sadie.

"Don't talk so daft. If he wanted me he wouldn't let the cost of a stamp stop him." Kevin subsided. "Sorry, Sadie love, I didn't mean to shout. It was just that I—"

Yes, Sadie knew.

"Weren't we the stupidist eejits thinking that jobs were there to be lifted just for the asking?"

There was nothing else for it now but to apply for several more. Kevin got hold of some national farming magazines which he studied carefully. It was no longer a question of deciding to stay in Cheshire, which both of them would have preferred. Now they would be grateful to get anything, anywhere.

"Well, almost anywhere," said Sadie. "Not Ireland though." She spoke jokingly.

Kevin looked up at her. "Why not Ireland?"

"You ask me why not? Surely to goodness it's obvious."

"Maybe we couldn't go back to Belfast or the North itself, but—"

"You don't mean to say you're thinking of the Republic?"

"Why not?" demanded Kevin. "Why not, Sadie? Sure there's Gerald in County Cork doing rightly."

"That's all very well, Gerald doing rightly. But he's not us. He has no wife, no Protestant wife."

"There's plenty Protestants live in the South. And many of them are happy enough."

"So *you* say. I've never met any of them myself."

"Your trouble is you're so prejudiced you wouldn't give anything new a chance."

"*I'm* prejudiced? What about yourself? How would you like it if I asked you to come and live in the middle of a bunch of Orangemen?" She tossed her head. Her temper was mounting.

Kevin was getting exasperated with her. He said it wasn't the same thing at all to ask her to come and live in the South of Ireland as it would be if she was to ask him to live in a community of Orangemen. Not all Catholics in the South were for the I.R.A., most of them wanted to live happily side by side with their Protestant neighbours. Sadie had the whole thing out of proportion.

"Sure I'm glad to hear it's me who has the whole thing out of proportion. Anyway, I'm not for going there myself to find out whether the Catholics would have me or not."

"Why not?" Kevin demanded again. "Why not?" It could make sense in many ways: he was more likely to pick up a job on a farm there, and they would be back in their own country at any rate. Sadie declared hotly that it was not *her* country, she would not feel at home.

"You weren't really thinking seriously of it, were you?"

Kevin sighed. "I was. But I must have been a bit soft in the head. I might have known how you'd go on if I suggested it."

He left the house, and from the kitchen window Sadie watched him striding across the fields. He had his hands in his pockets and his head down. Her anger died. He was the kindest, bravest man she had ever met, and she knew that all he wanted was to do the best he could by her and Brendan. She knew too that he would like very much to go back to Ireland, that he had never ceased to feel in exile here. But she could not go herself, not yet anyway. Perhaps sometime she might. But not yet. She could not even explain it fully to herself; it was something she felt in her bones rather than knew in her head. Kevin would tell her she had been conditioned by her upbringing, by all the stories of the wickednesses of priests and nuns, and how the church in Rome was out to grab you into its folds. She always told him that he had been conditioned too. By the tales his father had told. It took a long time to get rid of all the things you were brought up with, if you ever did.

Brendan was crawling around the floor between her feet. She looked down and saw that he had found an old bone of Tamsin's which he was chewing on happily. She grabbed the bone from him, which made him send up a howl of rage. Swiftly she gathered him into her arms, swinging him around to make him laugh and forget his loss.

"I'm not going to let you grow up with all these funny notions, Brendan my boy. You can make up your own mind about things. You will, won't you, eh?"

He would only be able to make up his mind up to a point, for she had had to agree that he would be brought up in the Catholic Church. From time to time this still made her uneasy, and she wondered what the outcome would be. It made no difference yet since Brendan was young and knew nothing about it, but as he grew older, what then?

After an hour Kevin came back. They kissed one another, without saying anything.

Kevin applied for five jobs, one in Cheshire, another in Shropshire, another in Yorkshire, another in Lancashire, and the fifth in Gloucestershire.

"I hope you get the one in Cheshire," said Sadie, crossing fingers on both hands.

"I just hope I get one."

He wrote more fully in these applications, with Sadie egging him on to sing his praises a little higher. She said he had got to push himself a bit more and he agreed. It was difficult to ask Mr Maxton to write five letters so they asked him for one which Kevin took to Chester and had photostatted.

Kevin laid the five envelopes on the kitchen table and Sadie stuck on the stamps. She banged the last one with her fist.

"Five different counties. It's a bit like a lucky dip. Isn't it funny how much of your life is due to accidents? I mean, our life is going to be different depending on which one of these comes up."

Or if none, thought Kevin, but did not say it.

"Perhaps we're always going to be on the move," she said. "Like gypsies."

"I hope not."

"Ah, come on! You're not an ould man yet."

"Times I feel it."

There must be some way of making life less of a lucky dip, thought Kevin, of being able to control your own fate. Hostages to fortune: that was what they were. That thought had been running in his mind continuously since Mr Ellersley's death. And the only way he could think to relieve that state of affairs would be if they could buy their own place. But how could they ever do that?

The letters were sent off, and this time Sadie resolved not to wait for the postman, although she couldn't help but lift her head more eagerly every time she heard his van approaching in the mornings. Kevin said it would take some days to get any replies at all and they must not count on anything.

On the day before his birthday, Brendan took his first step. Sadie was sitting in the living room reading a magazine when she looked up and saw him balancing on his two pudgy feet, with one hand against the settee. Suddenly he lurched forward and took two clear steps completely unaided.

"Kevin," shrieked Sadie, making Brendan waver and fall with a heavy plump on his round bottom. "Brendan can walk."

Kevin came running from the garden thinking a calamity had occurred.

"Brendan can walk! At least he took two steps."

She picked him up and stood him on his feet and put one hand on the settee. He stood there eyeing them, his dark eyes cheeky with laughter.

"Come on then, Brendan," said Sadie. "Show your Da what a clever boy you are." She held out her hands to him.

He lurched forward once more. One, two, three steps. And then he collapsed again.

They were thrilled. Sadie declared that he was very advanced for his age. As she picked the baby up and gave him a hug she felt happy right through to the middle. How funny it was to feel so happy when you knew that in a month's time you might have no home and no job! But at that moment it did not seem to matter.

The following morning, Brendan's birthday, the postman's van stopped. It was Kevin who went down the path to take the letters. He returned smiling.

"There's one with a Shropshire postmark."

He ripped it open quickly, took out a sheet of paper. It was an answer to his application, asking that he should come for an interview in a week's time.

"Hurrah!" shouted Sadie, doing a little jig round the room.

"Now don't get too carried away, Sadie. This isn't the offer of a job you know."

But once they saw Kevin, Sadie was convinced they would have no other person.

It was a busy morning for her: cooking, cleaning the house, and sprucing Brendan up for the big occasion. He was not one bit interested in getting dressed up and would have preferred to crawl around the earth in the garden. She tried to keep him in his playpen in the living room, without success, for he had found a way of vaulting neatly over the top. She told him that he never gave her a moment's peace, and that she could see that in the future he would give her less and less.

Fortunately, his birthday had fallen on a Saturday, which made it easier for people to come. After lunch, they began to arrive. First of all, from Manchester, came Kitty and Bill with their son David. Sadie rushed out to meet them, talking sixty to the dozen to Kitty, and behind her, crawling along the path in his clean blue smock, came Brendan. By the time the others appeared, Brendan was grubby but happy.

Mr Fiske brought in his van his wife, Mrs Hignett who kept the little corner shop in Liverpool where Sadie used to buy her messages, Maria Paradise and her mother and her two youngest sisters, Donna and Crystal.

"What a houseful," said Sadie happily. "Why haven't you all come before?"

"Ah well, Sadie, it takes us a while to get round to things," said

Mrs Hignett. "But now we know the way you can count on us to come again. You've a lovely wee place here."

Then Sadie told them that unfortunately they would not be able to come and visit them here again. Everyone lamented loudly, saying what a terrible shame it was.

"But never mind," said Sadie. "You can come to visit us in Shropshire. It's not that much further away. Only the next county."

"Now then, Sadie!" said Kevin. "We don't know yet if we're going to Shropshire or not."

Of course they were! On this golden August day, with all her friends around her and Brendan gurgling happily and filthily in their midst, Sadie felt that everything good was possible; not only possible, but highly likely.

"My, isn't he the loveliest babe?" said Mrs Paradise, swooping Brendan up into her arms and holding him against her plump bosom. Her dark eyes rolled at him. "I could just take you home with me. But sure I don't know what Mr Paradise would say." She shook with laughter.

"He mightn't be too happy," said Kevin. "I expect he has enough at home already."

There were seven Paradises and they lived in three rooms in a dilapidated house in a dilapidated part of Liverpool. Mr Paradise was in and out of work, mostly out, and now Maria had had to leave school to help support the family. She was an easy-going pleasant girl, who never seemed to take offence at anything her family asked. Sadie knew that she herself would never have been able to put up with the things that Maria did.

Sadie walked in the field for a few minutes with her.

"I had a letter from Gerald," said Maria shyly. They had been friends while Gerald was here and Sadie had been hoping for a big romance. "He seems to have settled in well back home."

Sadie still hoped that something might come of it between Gerald and Maria though Kevin thought there was little chance. There were too many things separating them, they were young, of different colour, and neither had any money. It was probably better, in Kevin's opinion, that Gerald had gone away and left

Maria before it had become too serious. "You men!" Sadie always ended up saying when they discussed Gerald and Maria. "Sure you have no romance in your souls." And then she would say that that was not strictly true for hadn't he run off with her? He reminded her that she had run off with him, but added that he was kind of glad that she had.

They had a picnic birthday tea in the garden. Sadie and Maria spread out all the sandwiches, sausage rolls, cakes, biscuits and trifles that Sadie had made.

"What a feast!" said Mrs Paradise. "Fit for the Queen herself."

"You're a grand wee baker, Sadie," said Mrs Hignett. "I never imagined it somehow."

They sat in a big circle on the grass around the tablecloth. The sun shone all afternoon, and after they had finished eating, the adults lay back and sunbathed. Brendan and David explored the garden and one another, never at rest for a moment.

"Don't know how they have the energy," murmured Kitty.

Sadie had not seen Kitty for months so they had a lot of news to catch up on. Kitty had a part-time job in the mornings whilst her mother looked after David. They were saving for a new fridge. They were always saving for something. Sadie thought that Kitty must have a long list which she kept ticking off. Washing machines, refrigerators, hi-fi machine, and so on. The list was probably endless. And they had a nice neat semi with a through lounge/dining-room, whilst she, Sadie—What did she have? She had Kevin and Brendan: that was a lot. Compared with them, refrigerators and hi-fis meant nothing. And she had Tamsin too, their lovely golden retriever, who was also running eagerly all over the garden and the people stretched out on the grass. No one minded, except perhaps Mrs Hignett who was unused to dogs and to the countryside itself, in fact. It was an unusual experience for her to lie on grass in sun. She seldom surfaced from her little shop where she spent the days and evenings in amongst newspapers, packets of soap powder, firelighters, packets of tights, cigarettes and almost everything else you could name. She said it was great this, lying here doing nothing in the fresh air; she must do it more often.

Sadie had also asked Mrs Hughes, Mrs Willis and Mrs Jones to look in, which they did. They came bearing yet more presents for Brendan.

"What a lucky boy you are, Brendan," said Sadie.

Brendan was more interested in David and the Paradise girls than his presents. Donna and Crystal made a real pet of him and staggered around the garden with him clutched like a pillow in their arms. He loved every moment of it.

It was a grand day! So said everyone. As the sun was dropping like a ball of fire behind the trees, Sadie and Kevin waved their guests off. Against Kevin's shoulder lay Brendan, sleeping, thumb tucked in at the corner of his mouth, head collapsed over his father's back.

"Come and visit us in Shropshire," called Sadie. "We'll send you our new address."

They promised that they would, no matter where Sadie and Kevin ended up.

"Even if it's Land's End," said Mrs Hignett.

"Or John O'Groats," added Maria, with a laugh.

Mr Fiske said that he would drive the Liverpool contingent, Sadie and Kevin could rely on that. Everyone declared that they would never forget Brendan's first birthday. Sadie and Kevin made promises too to visit them, in Manchester and in Liverpool.

"Goodbye," cried Sadie and Kevin. "Goodbye! And thanks for coming."

The cars drove away.

"Well," said Kevin, "I wonder where we'll be for the wee fella's second birthday?"

"Shropshire," said Sadie confidently. "I was talking to Mrs Hughes about it and she said we would like it. The part we're going to is very pretty apparently."

"You're half way there already, aren't you?"

They carried Brendan into the house and up the stairs, and laid him in his cot, just as he was, face and hands unwashed, and fully one year old.

Chapter Four

KEVIN went off to Shropshire for his interview, Sadie stayed at home with Brendan. She would have liked to have gone with Kevin so that she could have seen for herself what the new place looked like but it would have been too complicated. It was out of the question to take Brendan with them: he was at the stage when there was no peace to be had whilst he was awake and it was essential that Kevin should not be flustered in any way. Not that he often was, under any circumstances, for it was not his way, but Brendan would have put an extra strain on the proceedings. And it was rather a lot to ask Mrs Willis and Mrs Jones to take him for a whole day.

"You're a great fat nuisance at times," Sadie told Brendan as she fed him strained fish and macaroni at lunch time. He was trying to get both hands into the bowl. He sat in his high chair in the kitchen with his bare plump feet dangling, looking like an advertisement for healthy babies. The back door was wide open, letting the sun and air blow freely in.

Sadie looked out at the garden. At this time of year the greenery was thick and heavy. She could smell mint and lavender. Dear, but she loved this place! Her throat tightened at the thought of leaving it.

Brendan was shouting for more and banging his hands on the

table top. She turned back to him, lifting another spoonful into his open mouth. He was like a baby bird.

In the afternoon he crawled and tottered round the garden. He was taking a few more steps each day, gradually gaining confidence, but after four or five staggers, he would tire and resort to all fours. His speed on hands and knees was wild. Sadie spent the afternoon rescuing the flowers from his clutches and trying to pull up weeds herself.

"If you'd only stick to weeds too, Brendan!"

But flowers appealed more.

The long summer afternoon droned by. Sadie had never known such a long day, not that she could remember. Kevin had said he thought he would not be back till evening.

She gave Brendan his tea and bath in the garden. He had a marvellous time splashing water far and wide, hooting with laughter every time he hit his mother or Tamsin. The dog ran excitedly in circles around the blue plastic basin. It had been Brendan's bath since he was a small baby: now he was too large for it and filled it from side to side. It would do for the new baby. She must tell Kevin about the baby soon.

Brendan roared with fury when lifted from the water. He kicked and struggled and went turkey-cock red in the face.

"You're a right devil!"

Sadie wrapped him firmly in a towel and carried him inside. He looked so like Kevin that she was convinced he must be the spitting image of him as a baby and she almost wished that his granny in Tyrone could have come to see him. Almost. But not quite, for Kevin's mother had no time for her. She would have been so happy if Kevin had only married a nice Catholic girl and stayed beside his family in Tyrone.

Brendan finally asleep, Sadie sat by the sitting room window watching the shadows lengthen on the road. The sun went, dusk began to creep in amongst the trees.

She heard a bus coming, saw its lights. Its engine was slowing. She ran out in time to see Kevin alighting. His face looked lighter than it had done for a while.

"Well? Tell me quickly!"

"Hang on a minute. Let me get inside at least."

They went into the sitting-room and sat on the settee.

"Did you get it then?"

"I don't know yet."

"You don't know? Didn't the man say then?"

"He said he'd let me know. But I got on well with him, I could tell that. He was a nice man."

"And the place? What was the place like?"

"I think you'd like it. It's not unlike this house and there's a garden too with fields at the back."

Sadie leaned back. "Thank goodness!"

"But you mustn't count on it yet, Sadie. He was having another man come in three days' time for an interview too. He'll have to choose between us."

Another man! Sadie did not like the sound of that. But then she cheered again, for after all how could anyone prefer another man to Kevin, and hadn't the man liked Kevin a lot? Kevin *must* get this job.

He was tired. He let his head loll back against the settee. He told her about the farm, the number of livestock they had, the crops they grew and a little bit about some of the other workers. The farmer had taken him all over, showing him the barns, and the fields, and introducing him to the other people.

"Sounds like he was real serious then," said Sadie. "Otherwise he wouldn't have bothered, would he?"

Kevin said that they must wait now; the farmer would write after he had seen the other man. Sadie calculated that if the other man came in three days and the farmer wrote the day after then they could expect a letter in five days' time. It was better to reckon six or seven, said Kevin, you couldn't rely on the post that much, and besides, the farmer might not send the letter first class, now that postal rates were so high.

For the next few days Kevin went about his work as usual, saying little to anyone about the new job, but feeling fairly confident at the same time that he had a very good chance. He had clicked with the farmer, from the first moment of meeting. It happened that way with some people; it was quite unpredictable. He could sense that Sadie was simmering with excitement underneath but doing her best not to mention the subject to him. He had said it would be better if they left the matter alone now; there was nothing further to be done until news came. He had letters back from Gloucestershire and Lancashire saying that they were sorry but the jobs were filled. There was no word from the two other places. It had to be the Shropshire job: that was evident.

A letter came on the seventh morning. He brought it into the house and sat down at the kitchen table to open it. Sadie stood behind him looking over his shoulder.

He slit the envelope open, took out the single sheet of paper. He began to read, and almost immediately his face changed and he moved the letter out of Sadie's sight.

"What is it?" she cried. "Kevin, haven't you got the job after all?"

"I'm afraid not," he said bluntly, laying the paper on the table. "He says he's terribly sorry but the other man turned out to have ten years' experience and he felt he couldn't turn him down. He wishes me all the best."

"All the best!" cried Sadie. "A fat lot of use that is! Why couldn't he just have given you the job? Why, why, why?"

Kevin sat with his elbows on the table, his head supported between his hands. He said that it was fair enough, with the other man having so many years' experience behind him, while he himself had had less than one year.

"It's not fair enough, it's not!"

Sadie ranted for a bit, then collapsed into tears. Kevin got up and put his arms round her and stroked her hair.

"Don't worry, Sadie love. We've had troubles before and we've got over them. We'll get over this one, you'll see."

It was then she spilled out the news about the baby, telling him quite differently from the way she had intended. She had gone over in her head what she would say, had decided to break it to him gently; and she had wanted to sound calm and unbothered, as if she was taking everything in her stride.

"Another baby?"

"Aren't you even pleased about it? We're going to have another baby and you don't even want it!" Sadie knew that she was being unreasonable, even whilst she was saying it but could not help it. She needed to lash out.

Kevin said in a shattered voice that of course he would like the new baby, it was just that it was coming at the wrong time. When was it due? The end of January, she told him. The end of January! The worst time of year. When the weather was bad and spring never seemed to be coming. It was a dead time of year, one that you always wanted to get over as fast as possible.

"And we'll have no house for the child to be brought home to. What are we going to do, Kevin?"

"I'll need to think. I don't know."

He could easily get work at a number of farms in the area but there were no houses going. It might be necessary for them to find rooms somewhere, perhaps in Chester, and for him to travel to work every day. They didn't want to go back to that, renting a couple of tatty rooms, said Sadie; she wanted a place of her own. Like this one.

"I know, love. But if we can't get that then at least I must get work."

She dried her eyes and said that she was sorry to be crying like a baby. Gently, he told her she was silly, she could cry whenever she wanted to.

During the next few days he did a lot more thinking. He studied the houses for sale in the local papers and felt a bit of a fool even to be doing it for the prices were miles out of their reach. They only had a hundred and fifty pounds in all! And no building society would be dying for the chance to give them a mortgage. After all, wasn't he soon to be jobless? He talked also to Mr Maxton who was unable to suggest anything other than watching the papers for jobs. Kevin would find something, he felt sure, given time. But time was something that Kevin did not have. In not much more than a week they were due to leave the cottage, and Mr Allan did not look the kind of man who would take pity on them and give them an extension. He had been out at the farm again, striding about, puffing his cigar, his sharp eyes darting this way and that, but he had not seemed much interested in any of the human beings around. It was the land that interested him, and the money to be made from the land. No, Kevin knew that come the end of August, they must pack up their stuff and move on.

He went after one other job in mid-Cheshire, but arrived too late, for someone got there before him.

"I'm thinking we might have to resort to a caravan, Sadie. Just in the meantime. What would you think of that?"

A caravan? Sadie made a face, not fancying it much at all, not in comparison with this little cottage, with three bedrooms upstairs and two rooms down, and the garden full of flowers and the smell of mint and lavender.

"Beggars can't be choosers, I suppose."

It was thinking about a caravan that led Kevin on to the next thing: a caravette, a car for them to travel around in and sleep in at the same time. If he bought a caravan he couldn't afford a car.

"A caravette?" said Sadie. "But aren't they awfully small inside?"

Kevin admitted that they were, but it could be a useful thing to have, it would mean they could tour the countryside and he could take jobs wherever he could find them. Sadie thought about it for a moment.

"It might be rather exciting," she said slowly. "We'd really be like gypsies, wouldn't we?" she giggled. "You look a bit Romany, you know. But what about our furniture? What would we do with it?"

"We could get rid of most of it. It's not worth much, is it? And anything we do want to keep we can store at the pub. I've already spoken to Mr Hughes and he says he wouldn't mind. I know it doesn't seem much, Sadie, to take in exchange for a house, but maybe it's the only thing we can do at the moment. We have to sleep somewhere."

The more Sadie thought about it the more she liked the idea. But as a thing to live in forever, certainly not, and certainly not still to be in in the middle of winter when she would give birth to her baby, but as a stop-gap it might not be a bad thing at all. They could even treat it like a bit of a holiday. She had always fancied going to Wales, or down to Cornwall, or even up to Scotland.

Kevin laughed. "Now you're letting the whole thing run away with you again! Before we know it you'll be having us heading for Timbuctoo."

"Might not be such a bad idea after all. Timbuctoo, I mean. If we've got to go at all we might as well go in style."

Kevin went with George to look at second-hand caravettes. They found one on the third day of looking, in quite good condition, considering its age and the amount of money he paid for it. Rather proudly, for he had never owned a motor vehicle in his life, Kevin drove it back from Chester along the country roads, through the village, down past the wall of the Ellersley Hall estate to their cottage. He drew up outside their front door and tooted the horn.

The front door flew open, out came Sadie running. Behind her staggered Brendan waving his hands, shouting indecipherable sounds, but conveying the impression that his mother should wait for him. She did not wait, she had her eyes on the red and cream bus in front of the gate.

Kevin slid open the window. "Your new home, madam."

"Hey, it's great, Kev!" Her eyes were shining.

He smiled at her. She was never one to be down for long, she always found a bright side to look on, and was ready to take a chance. Sure wasn't that why she had married him in the first place?

Sadie remembered Brendan, turned and swooped him up before he crawled under the van. Kevin leaned across and opened the passenger door.

"All aboard then! Shall I take you for a ride in your new house?"

Sadie sat up beside Kevin with Brendan on her knee. Before they set off she fastened the safety belt across both her and the boy. He was trying to grab everything in sight, from the steering wheel to the road tax sticker on the windscreen.

"Sit still, lump!" said Sadie. "We're going for a ride with your da. Gosh, Kevin, isn't it high up sitting here?" The seats were much higher than in an ordinary car. She liked it for it gave her a better view of the world.

Kevin put the car into gear, started the engine, and off they went for their first drive in their new travelling home.

Chapter Five

"YOU'RE going to be living in a *bus?*" said Mrs Willis. "Mercy!"

"I wouldn't have thought that'd be very suitable for a small child," said Mrs Jones.

"It's just temporary like, of course," said Sadie.

Mrs Willis sighed. "Ah well, you didn't have much choice, did you, lass?"

Mrs Willis and Mrs Jones were not all that happy themselves: the more they saw of Mr Allan the less they liked him. They had a feeling that it would not be long before they themselves were moving on.

"Maybe you could spare us a seat in your bus, Sadie," said Mrs Jones, and they laughed at the idea of them all squashed into the vehicle.

It might be rather a lark, thought Sadie, but Kevin probably wouldn't fancy it. Two adults, one baby and a dog would be enough to be getting on with. As she dusted she sang, thinking of all the marvellous places they might go to. She and Mr Ellersley had had many a good chat about Wales and Scotland and the Yorkshire Dales. He was a man who had enjoyed hills and dales and rugged coastlines. He had given her several maps which she was going to look out that day when she went home.

The thought of maps and the Welsh hills were so much in her

mind that she did not notice the car parked outside their gate until she was almost on top of it. It was a long, shiny, red one, which she had never seen before. It did not belong to anyone they were likely to know. She saw that a man and woman were sitting in the front staring ahead. Suddenly, they must have noticed her in the mirror, for the passenger door opened and out got the woman. She turned and looked at Sadie.

"Well, Sadie Jackson! It is you, isn't it Sadie? You haven't changed."

Sadie stood and stared at her, not recognising her. She frowned.

"Don't you remember me then? Linda. Linda Mullet."

Linda Mullet! Of course Sadie remembered her, they had played together as children, had been brought up in the same street in Belfast until Sadie had left to go off with Kevin. And this was Linda Mullet? She had her hair set up in waves as Sadie's own mother might have hers done, and she was wearing a pink Crimplene suit with a frilly blouse showing beneath. She looked almost middle-aged, thought Sadie.

The driver's door opened, and out got the man. He was of middle height, but very broad across the shoulders and very thick around the waist.

"This here is Ollie, my husband," said Linda. "We've just got married, we're on our honeymoon. I'm Mrs McGibbon now."

Ollie stood and grinned at Sadie; he clearly seemed delighted to be just married, and to Linda. Sadie muttered her congratulations, still not quite able to take it in that it was Linda Mullet who was standing there in front of her in the road in a pink Crimplene suit and frilly blouse. She hadn't set eyes on Linda for about three years.

"Your mother gave me your address," said Linda. "We thought we'd just look you up like, on our way south."

"Oh yes, yes, I'm glad you've come," said Sadie hurriedly, adding, "Won't you come in then?"

She pushed Brendan up the garden path; they followed. It was only then that she remembered the mess she had left inside that day, for the night before they had been packing their stuff into boxes to be stored at the Hughes'. The house was like a pigsty and the thought of Linda Mullet seeing it and going back home to give a full report up and down their old street made Sadie want to turn and run. But there was nothing else for it but to put the key in the lock and open the door.

"Come away in," she said, tossing her hair back proudly. She had nothing to be ashamed of where Linda Mullet was concerned, and she couldn't care less now what the street would think of her. They thought enough things already, just because she was married to a Catholic. Their street was Protestant to the last man.

She took them into the sitting-room which now only had two chairs left in it. The rest of the space was taken up with packing cases and cardboard boxes.

"Are you leaving then?" asked Linda. "Looks like a flittin'."

"Yes, we're moving," said Sadie. "Take a seat, and I'll put the kettle on."

Linda took a seat, looking distastefully at it before she put her pink Crimplene bottom into it as if it might contain snakes. Ollie collapsed into the other chair, still smiling. He seemed to do little else but smile. Sadie lifted Brendan out of his push-chair and deposited him in the middle on the floor. He took one look at Linda and Ollie and rushed for Sadie's legs.

"Seems like he's a bit strange with people," said Linda.

"He isn't normally," said Sadie. "He's usually right friendly."

Brendan followed Sadie into the kitchen where she put the kettle on the gas and set three cups on a tray. Then she raked in her biscuit tins desperately searching for half a dozen whole biscuits. Five was as many as she could find, and she gave a few of the odds and ends to Brendan to keep him happy. He had been in a slightly crabby mood all morning; she thought he was cutting a tooth. What a day for Linda Mullet of all people to arrive! It was funny to have her arrive at all, for Sadie had never expected to see her again.

She carried the tray of tea-things back into the room where Linda and Ollie were sitting as she had left them. They did not seem to have exchanged a word in her absence. Ollie was smiling; Linda's eyes were roving the room, taking in every detail.

"Not a bad wee place you have here," said Linda.

46

"We like it very much. Do you take milk and sugar in your tea, Ollie?"

"I do that. Three sugars if you don't mind."

Sadie poured the tea, handed it out and offered the biscuits. Linda declined, saying that she was watching her figure, but Ollie took two. Sadie squatted on top of a box.

"Why are you leaving then?" asked Linda. "Seeing as you like it."

"We just fancied a change, that's all."

"Your mother didn't say anything about it."

"She doesn't know yet. I'll be writing her tomorrow."

"Where are you off to?"

"We're not sure."

"You're not sure? Haven't you got a new place then?"

"Oh, we've two or three things on offer, it's just that we're not sure yet which one we'll take. Kevin fancies Shropshire, but I like the idea of Gloucestershire myself."

Linda paused for a moment to take a drink of tea. Her eyes were as sharp as a tack, thought Sadie, just like her mother's had been. Her mother used to spend the day leaning on her door jamb making sure that she missed nothing that happened in the street. Mrs Mullet in rollers and fur slippers lounging against the wall! Lord, the thought of that took her back!

"We've got a lovely little bungalow up the Lisburn Road," said Linda, primping up the back of her hair with her hand. "It's got three bedrooms, sitting-room, and dining-room. Detached. And there's quite a big garden too, isn't there, Ollie?"

Ollie grunted, assenting that there was. Sadie refilled his cup, offered him the biscuit plate again.

"Ollie's a bookmaker," said Linda with pride. "He's in business with his father."

"I hope you'll enjoy living up the Lisburn Road then," said Sadie, and added, with a little grin, unable to resist it, "It'll be quite a change for you, won't it, Linda? Having a garden and that?"

Linda flushed under the roots of her corrugated hair. Sadie knew that perhaps it wasn't a very nice thing to have said, but Linda

Mullet didn't make her feel very nice. It was funny, but the return of Linda almost seemed to have brought back the feelings that Sadie had had when she was growing up in the street, and a way of acting and talking. There had always been a bit of sharpness between them. Bitchiness, Kevin would have called it. It was just as well he was not here to listen to it.

Brendan clambered up on to Sadie's knee and clung to her. He had two fingers in the corner of his mouth and was slavering a little. Sadie explained that he was a very happy baby but today was cutting teeth. Linda looked as if she did not believe it, as if she thought that Brendan was one of the most irritating babies she had ever clapped eyes on.

"More tea?" asked Sadie, willing them to get up and depart. She did not want them to be here when Kevin returned home from work; he had no happy memories of Linda, or of Sadie's street, for that matter. But they showed no signs of going. Linda refused tea, dusted off her pink skirt and put the cup on the floor by her feet. Ollie said that he wouldn't mind some more if there was any going, so Sadie got up and refilled the kettle.

"Ollie's a terrible tea man," said Linda. Everything she said, was made to sound like an asset, and a unique one at that.

Ollie wore a brightly checked suit which looked too thick and hot for the month of August and new shiny tan shoes and bright yellow socks. He was a dazzling sight to behold sure enough, thought Sadie, and giggled inside herself, wishing that she had someone she would be able to tell the story to afterwards. That was something she still missed, having a friend to gossip with. It was not that she didn't talk to Kevin, but it wasn't the same as talking to a girl-friend. Once she and Linda had been close, had talked everything over, but that had been in the earlier days of their childhood. As they grew up they had grown apart.

Thinking of their childhood, Sadie began to ask about people they had known in their district in Belfast, and for an hour or so she and Linda chatted, forgetting for a while that they were now married women, in different situations, living out differing lives. Sadie enjoyed hearing what had happened to this one and that one. Do you remember? They found they remembered a lot, and from time to time giggled as they recalled the devilment they had got up to in their younger days. Sadie, glancing sideways at Ollie, saw that he slept, hands clasped peacefully in his lap.

And then they ran out of gossip. For a time there was silence in the little room. Even Brendan was sleeping, snuggled against Sadie's breast, fingers resting loosely against his mouth. Sadie and Linda eyed one another. They looked, and looked away.

"Oh, I've just remembered!" said Linda. "Your mother gave me some things for the baby."

For a moment Sadie started, thinking that Linda meant the new baby, but of course it was of Brendan she was speaking. Linda roused Ollie who went to the car and came back with a large parcel.

Sadie undid the parcel and took out a heap of knitted garments that her mother must have laboured over by her fire in the kitchen. All of them were too small for Brendan. Jumpers, cardigans, trousers, socks.

"Sure those wouldn't do for him at all," said Linda. "He's far too big for them."

"No, but they'll do for the—" Sadie stopped.

"Are you expecting again then? For dear sake! Of course, I suppose you would, being married to a Mick." Linda smiled and went on, "No offence meant, I'm sure." But she did not look one bit sorry to have said it, and Sadie's temper flared.

"You've no call to come here saying a thing like that, Linda Mullet!"

"I said no offence meant."

"But I don't like the word!"

"Mick?" Linda rolled her eyes. "But he is one, isn't he?"

Brendan, wakened, began to grizzle, shoving his fist further into his mouth. Sadie, rattled, and irritated herself now, rocked him and spoke soothingly. She wished again that Linda and Ollie would get up and go.

There was another silence, broken this time by Ollie.

"Sure it's very nice here, Sadie," said Ollie. "I like England myself. I've nothing against it."

Neither Linda nor Sadie paid any attention to him, but he did not seem to mind. The two girls were taken up totally with one another. Back in Belfast they had fallen out because Sadie had kept company with Kevin: that had been the final rift between them. So why had Linda come now to look her up? It was unlikely that it was because she was sorry for her attitude then. Sadie thought rather that she couldn't resist coming to show off her fancy new car and talk about her fancy bungalow on the Lisburn Road. As if Sadie cared about bungalows and shiny cars!

"Shush, Brendan love, shush," she said.

He stood up on her knee, pushing his hot cheek against her face.

"Your mother doesn't know about this next baby then, does she?"

"No, not yet. I'll be writing to her about that and all."

"She was saying that she was thinking of coming over this autumn to see you. She'd like to see Brendan again."

Sadie flinched at the idea of another visit from her mother. They had had one last autumn in Liverpool and that had been bad enough, although in the end she had been glad her mother had come to see her baby. But this year it would not do at all, especially since they would have nowhere to put her. Imagine her mother on one of the bunks in the caravette!

Ollie yawned, spread his tan and yellow feet out in front of him.

"Are you going far today?" asked Sadie.

They were not fussy about travelling too much in a day, said Linda; they thought they might just put up somewhere round about. Ollie observed again that he thought it was nice round here, that he liked England. "No, I've nothing against it." Sadie thought he must be a bit soft in the head.

"Would you like to see the garden?" she asked, in desperation to get out into the fresh air.

Linda said she didn't mind. She got up, Ollie stayed where he was, his eyelids beginning to droop again, and the two girls went into the garden with Brendan. Linda was not particularly interested in the flowers though she said again they had a lovely garden attached to their bungalow on the Lisburn Road. They were going to have a man come in once a week to do it.

"Ollie'd give me anything I wanted," she said, nodding back

towards the cottage where Ollie was presumably slumbering in peace. "He's dead generous. Says I can have a woman in to clean too if I want. And I'm not to go out working or anything like that."

Sadie did not reply. She had known Linda Mullet too long and too well to have to observe the niceties with her. She gazed out across the fields and wondered when Kevin would be coming home. They sat on the garden seat and half closed their eyes against the sun. At least it was better out in the open air with Linda than in the box-littered room. Linda chattered on about her bungalow, about the suites and carpets and curtains and kitchen equipment. She, like Sadie, had grown up in a terraced back-to-back, with no garden or fancy kitchen equipment.

"It's just like a little palace," she said, echoing her mother. And Sadie's mother. Sadie's mother's dream would be for Sadie to have a little palace of her own.

Sadie put Brendan down on the grass to play with Tamsin, and for a little while the baby forgot his mouth. He loved to play with the dog, who was gentle and careful with him. At one point Tamsin rushed towards Linda, jumping and placing her paws squarely on Linda's pink skirt. Linda shrieked, as if she'd been bitten.

"Just dust it off," said Sadie. "I'm sure it'll not leave a mark."

It was drip-dry anyway, said Linda, and she had two other suits with her. Ollie had insisted that she get herself a big trousseau and had given her the money for it himself.

The sun moved round, but Linda and Ollie did not move from the cottage. If they stayed much longer, thought Sadie, she would have to offer them tea. She could not be so inhospitable as to turn them away without food unless they offered to leave themselves. When it was nearing five they went back into the house to find that Ollie was deep asleep. They heard his snores from the back door.

"Sure he's dead tired," said Linda. "That driving fairly goes for you, so it does."

Just then, Sadie heard a car outside. Glancing out, she saw their red and cream bus pull up.

"Here's Kevin now."

Linda perked up, preened slightly and patted the sides of her hair with her hand, in the way that Sadie had often seen Mrs Mullet do in days gone by, especially when there was a man in the offing.

The door opened, in came Kevin. He stopped on the threshold, bewildered, not recognising either Linda or Ollie. He glanced enquiringly at Sadie.

"Don't you remember me, Kevin?" said Linda pertly. "Linda. Linda Mullet." Still Kevin frowned. The name meant nothing to him. "I lived in Sadie's street. We played together when we were kids. And you and I've fought one another, surely you remember that?"

"We only fought once," said Sadie.

The night they had fought, Kevin's sister Brede had been injured and nearly died. It was that night, and that fight, that had brought Sadie and Kevin together.

Ollie, wakened from sleep, struggled out of the chair to shake hands with Kevin. His face was now bright red and glistening.

"Heard a lot about you," he said. "'Deed I have. Linda's mother's always speaking about you and Sadie here."

They all sat down, and Sadie did not know what to do or say next. To be stuck for words was a new situation for her. Brendan was grumbling more and more, getting redder and redder in the cheek, and pulling at her for attention. It was Linda who did the talking now. As she prattled she looked only at Kevin now who sat on top of a box with his hands clasped around his knees. His eyes seemed glazed, as if his thoughts were far away. And indeed they were. He was thinking about the latest letter from his mother which Sadie had not seen. 'Can't you do anything about Clodagh for me, Kevin, son?' she had asked. She was always asking things of him, things that he could not give.

"Would you like to stay to tea?" said Sadie at last.

"Well, we don't want to put you out like," said Linda. "But we wouldn't mind, would we, Ollie?"

Ollie did not seem to mind anything as long as Linda wanted it. He said that'd be grand if it'd be no trouble, otherwise they could go out and find a restaurant. He could eat anything, he declared;

ham and eggs would do fine. He liked good simple food, nothing fancy.

"But we often go out and eat Chinese, don't we, Ollie?" put in Linda quickly.

"But I'd just as soon have ham and eggs."

In the kitchen Sadie had plenty of fresh, newly-laid eggs, but no bacon. She asked Kevin if he could go to the village and buy some. Whilst he was gone, she gave Brendan his tea and put him to bed. Linda followed her about the house, watching her feed the baby and wash his hands and face. Her eyes roved the kitchenette, the bathroom, Brendan's little attic bedroom.

Sadie cooked the bacon and eggs and set the table in the sitting-room. Then they all sat down to eat. It was one of the worst meals that Sadie had ever eaten in her life. The bacon was tough, the eggs hard, the tea stewed, and Linda never stopped talking. It still amazed Sadie that Linda was here at all, sitting at the table with Kevin, talking to him. It was something that she would not have done in Belfast. Ollie ate and drank and smiled, and from time to time said, "Boys, this is great. Nothing like a good plate of rashers. Just like me mother does them." No one ever seemed to answer him, and he never seemed to expect an answer.

"I hear you can't make up your mind which job to choose?" said Linda, looking at Kevin.

Sadie made a face at Kevin, trying to indicate that he should give nothing away. Linda, glancing sideways, got the message and smiled, cat-like. She dabbed her lips with her paper serviette. It was one left over from Brendan's birthday party.

"Are you pleased with your car, Ollie?" asked Kevin, turning to him.

"Oh aye, I am indeed. Right pleased. Would you like to see it?"

The men went out to examine the engine of Ollie's car, the women went to the kitchen. Sadie washed up and Linda leant against the draining board offering to dry but making no effort to lift a cloth. Then back to the sitting room they went again and sat down.

"Think we'll need to be moving, Linda," said Ollie, when he came in with Kevin. "I suppose you wouldn't know of a wee hotel nearby we could go, would you, Sadie?

"There's nothing round here," said Sadie quickly. "Your best bet would be to go into Chester. There's plenty of good hotels there."

Linda got up, rearranged her Crimplene skirt, and said they'd better be off then to make sure they got booked into a good hotel. None of those cheap bed and breakfast places for them! You never knew what you were getting into if you went into some of those houses.

"I'll tell everyone back home you were asking after them, will I?"

"Yes," said Sadie, "do that."

"Nice meeting you," said Ollie. "It's been good crack so it has."

Linda and Ollie McGibbon drove off in their shiny, long, red car, and Sadie and Kevin returned to their sitting room.

"That was dreadful, Kevin! I've had a desperate afternoon."

"Ach well, she's away now."

"But she'll go back and tell everybody about everything."

"How do you mean? Everything?"

Sadie waved her hand round the room. "This! The mess, and that we're moving and have nowhere to go to. They'll all be saying that they knew Sadie Jackson would come to no good in the end."

"Don't talk so daft. What do you care what they say over there anyway? Sure you're well away from it all."

"Yes, I am, aren't I? Well away." And Sadie burst into tears.

Kevin came and put his arms around her. "Oh, come on now, love, it was only Linda Mullet after all. I can see you've had a trying afternoon but she's nothing to us, is she?" He lifted Sadie's chin so that he could look into her face.

She grinned, dried her tears on the back of her arm. Of course he was right. Linda Mullet was of no importance whatsoever. But she did wish nevertheless that she hadn't bothered her head coming to pay them a visit.

"What a big silly lump she's married!" said Sadie.

"Seemed good-natured enough."

"He'd need to be, married to Linda Mullet!"

Chapter Six

THEIR last few days at the cottage slipped away quickly. They had much to do. Kevin went about preoccupied, his head spinning with thoughts. Sadie, now that she had accepted the move, was treating it as a big adventure and had got him to agree that they would take a week's holiday over in Wales first, before he started to look for work. He had written away for two other jobs.

He helped take the cows to market and watched them being sold and led off by their new owners. He'd miss them! Yes, he would, and walking across the fields in the early morning to the byre. Ah well, there'd be something else. There would have to be; he had a wife and child to provide for, and another coming. And he had yet another letter in his pocket from his mother. He sat on a bench in the Cathedral garden in Chester and read it again.

The letter had come the day before; he himself had collected it from the postman and had again said nothing to Sadie about it. Sometimes Kevin wished that they would not get any mail for about six months for most of the letters which came from his mother carried bad news. This one contained another appeal for him to come back, to come to Tyrone where he could get work on the farm where his mother and the rest of his family lived. Clodagh, who was fifteen, had run off, and there was no news of her. Kevin's mother said her burdens were heavy and that she had need of him. Sure wasn't he her eldest son and no one else could take his place? There was Gerald miles away in County Cork, and anyway, he wasn't of much use. But she did have Brede, Kevin reminded himself, and Brede was a good daughter to her, so she was not as alone as her letters made it sound. He had to harden his heart to her plea: he could not go.

And he could do nothing about Clodagh. It worried him of course but he had other worries of his own, more pressing worries. He remembered Clodagh as a lively child turning cartwheels in the street, but now that she was fifteen years old he could not begin to imagine what she would be like. He was growing apart from his family and he did not like that. Then he thought that he had another family now, his own, and this was the natural way of things.

It was something his mother could not seem to accept. He tried, when he wrote, to tell her, to explain but she could not, or would not, understand. If only he'd come home! It was always her cry. She seemed to think that everything in life would be smoothed out by his return.

Whilst he was in Chester he did some shopping, bought a few things they needed for the van. They were all but ready to go, everything was packed up, some things stored at the Hughes's, and everything else had either been given or thrown away.

Sadie was baking cakes when he came home. Opening the kitchen door he smelled the strong sweet aroma coming from the oven. It took him back to the little kitchen in the house in Belfast where his mother used to bake every Saturday, spending hours with her arms up to the elbows in flour, her face red from the heat of the stove, and the back door open on to the little yard to let in some air. Sadie's face was flushed and pink; she was baking for their farewell party.

They held it in the garden since there was nothing left to sit on in the house. It was a mild evening, and they sat on rugs on the grass. The Maxtons came, and the Hughes, Mrs Willis, Mrs Jones, Bobby, and Pauline and George. They had a good evening, and at the end of it Mr Maxton got to his feet rather solemnly, coughed, and made a little speech. He said that they were all sorry that Sadie and Kevin were leaving, he wished them well and then passed over an envelope to Kevin. Inside were ten pounds.

"That's from the lot of us," said Mr Maxton gruffly. "Couldn't think what to buy you, seeing as you're going off in a van, so we thought we'd let you get something for yourselves."

Sadie thought that she would burst into tears.

Next morning, the garden was quiet, except for the birds. They were up almost as soon as dawn broke, packing the last few things into boxes, putting them into the van. Sadie put Brendan and Tamsin into the garden to have a last run round. Not that either of them knew that it would be their last run here, not that possibly either of them would care if they did know. The dog barked happily, Brendan chattered to himself in his own language and went round picking heads off flowers. Automatically, Sadie checked him, telling him no, it was wrong to pick flowers, even though no one else would come and enjoy their garden. This part of the land would come into the building area. Their house, their garden, would be swept away by bulldozers and replaced by neat lines of houses.

"Ready then?" called Kevin. "Let's go."

Sadie gathered up Brendan and Tamsin and put them into the back of the red and cream van. Then she and Kevin went back to the house to take a last look round, to see that they had not missed anything.

"We were happy here, weren't we?" said Sadie. "But never mind, we'll be happy somewhere else."

They left the house, Kevin locking the door and putting the key under a stone where Mr Maxton would pick it up later. Hand-in-hand, they walked down the path together and got into their new home. Brendan was waving his arms around and flapping his bare feet. He at least was ready for off, wanted action.

At that time of morning the roads were quiet. Kevin drove smoothly and carefully along the country roads, through Chester, over the river Dee and across the border into Wales. A brand new country for both of them! Sadie had her map on her knee. She felt as if they were setting out to take on the world. She wouldn't mind a world tour, not one bit. But North Wales would do to be getting on with. The names intrigued her; she tried pronouncing them, laughing as she stumbled and floundered through the words. She said that she would never get the hang of words like that with all those double ls, fs and ds everywhere.

Mr Hughes had given them the name and address of his brother who also kept a pub; it was in a little village not very far over the border, a few miles from the town of Ruthven. Mr Hughes had said that he was sure his brother Tom would be pleased to see them, very pleased indeed. And so they thought they might as well stop off there for an hour and say hello.

"Those are the Clwyd Mountains ahead," said Sadie. The mountains were blue in the morning light, and the countryside glowed all around them in the sunshine. This country was different from Cheshire, much less populated for a start, and of course hillier. They had a feeling of escaping from civilisation as they bowled along the road, heading towards these blue hills. No doubt it was the reason that traffic went non-stop from the Midlands to North Wales all summer.

Before they reached the village where Mr Hughes's brother lived, they stopped and had a mid-morning snack, sitting on the grass outside the van. They went over a fence into a field so that Brendan and Tamsin were able to have a good run well away from the road.

"It's great being on holiday," said Sadie. "I've only ever had two holidays in my life."

Kevin said that he had never had any, they had never been able to afford things like that in their family. Sadie had been once to Bangor, a seaside resort twelve miles outside Belfast, and another time to Portrush, on the Antrim coast. She had gone with her mother and father and Tommy for a week, and they'd had a great time digging in the sand, building castles, paddling in the water, and going to visit the Giant's Causeway. That was a long time ago. She felt a stab thinking of Tommy. He wrote seldom from Australia and she could not imagine what his life would be like.

"We'll need to try and take holidays every year, Kev. I'm sure it's good for people to get away."

Kevin smiled, lay back on the grass with his hands clasped behind his head. The meadow smelt sweet, of buttercups and daisies, and of cows that were grazing in the next field. He loved the country, hoped he would never have to go back to the town, to dirty streets and reeking chimneys. He wanted—had hoped—to be finished with all of that.

Returning to the van, they proceeded to the village of Mr Hughes's brother. It had a big long name beginning with a double L that Sadie could not pronounce at all. The village nestled in the fold of the hills, tucked away out of the winds, but yet with a full clear view down the valley. It was a pretty village, built of Welsh stone, different again from their old village in Cheshire which had been mostly red-brick with some half-timbering. The pub was easily found, sitting as it did in the middle of the village. *The Speckled Hen*. It was an old sprawling building, covered with rambling roses and had a bit of a garden in front where three rather rickety tables stood. A few people sat round one of the tables in the garden drinking beer and eating sandwiches.

Mr Hughes's brother was behind the bar. He was delighted to meet them, shook hands and offered a drink. On the house, he said. They sat in the garden to drink it and let Brendan run about. It was a quiet village, hardly any cars passed through at all, and those that did did not go at speed. Business was quiet in the middle of the day, so Mr Hughes came to sit beside them, bringing his pint of beer.

They told him how his brother and his wife were, and he told them about the village. He had been in this pub for twenty years, knew everyone in the area like the back of his hand. He liked it here; the way of life suited him. He was no townsman. Some of the people in the village had lived here all their lives, others were incomers and commuted to work, some of them weekly, travelling as far as Manchester. There were only a few like that of course, and Mr Hughes did not seem to approve of them too much. He lived alone in the pub; his wife was dead now, and his only daughter had gone away to London. He spoke of it as if it was the moon.

A customer called; Mr Hughes excused himself. Sadie and Kevin got up and wandered down the road with Kevin carrying Brendan on his shoulders, and Tamsin running in front of them sniffing the ground, wagging her tail with enthusiasm. The hedge-rows were full of wild flowers and grasses. Trees spread shade over their heads as they walked.

"It's got a very nice feel, this place," said Sadie.

Kevin nodded. He liked tree-lined roads, and beyond roads, green fields, and beyond them, hills.

"Why don't we just spend the rest of the day here and the night too?" said Sadie. "I expect Mr Hughes would let us park the van at the side of the pub."

Kevin thought tht a good idea, he did not feel much like driving far that day and sure didn't they have all the time in the world? He grinned at her. A week at least. And that to them, with nothing to do but take their ease and enjoy themselves, was a lot of time.

They came to a low stone wall running along on their right with parkland rolling away behind it. Through some distant trees they could just make out the roofline of a house. Turning a corner, they saw a man sitting on the wall gazing over the park. When they reached him, he turned to look at them and smiled.

"Lovely day, isn't it?" said Sadie.

"Grand." The man called to Tamsin, flicking his fingers which brought the dog running. In a moment Tamsin was scrambling all over him and Sadie trying to pull him off. But no, the man said he didn't mind, he liked dogs. He'd never had one, he said, though he intended to now. He seemed to want to chat a bit so Sadie sat down on the wall beside him. He was a man in his fifties, she reck-oned, and he wore a city suit, so clearly he didn't belong in these parts. She began to chat to him, to tell him about Tamsin and how she had saved to buy her. Kevin swung Brendan down from his shoulders and let him sit on the wall beside Sadie. The man said what a fine boy he was, what bright dark eyes he had. There was a lilt in his voice that neither Sadie nor Kevin could fail to recognise.

"Are you from Ireland?" asked Kevin.

The man laughed. "A long time ago. A very long time. But I suppose you can still hear it, eh? You're from the old country yourselves, aren't you? I came over from Limerick—Oh, it must be thirty years ago, or more. I've lived my life in Birmingham since then. I set up in business there. And now I'm retiring, coming here." He nodded across the parkland at the distant trees.

"Do you mean here?" asked Sadie. "To that house?"

The man said that he had just bought it, and the land surrounding, about ten acres in all. He had always intended when he retired to return to Ireland but when it came to the bit he thought he had been too long away. His wife was Welsh, she had been brought up near here, so when they saw this little estate advertised they'd gone for it at once. He was retiring early, he'd decided he'd had enough of business and Birmingham, and he wanted some time to enjoy himself. Sadie told him that he was quite right, a man could work too long and by the time he stopped not be fit to enjoy anything. Kevin was amused at Sadie. She could give advice to businessmen from Birmingham without batting an eyelid, or in any way annoying them when she gave it.

They must have spent an hour talking to the man on the wall, looking out over the parkland at his house. They talked about Ireland and its problems, and Sadie told him the condensed story of their lives.

"It can't have been easy for you," he said, and then he asked if they would like to come and see his house. Immediately Sadie sprang off the wall, lifting Brendan with her. They set off across the smooth green grass between the large spreading oaks, coming to the clump of trees that sheltered the house. It was not a grand house in the way that Ellersley Hall had been, but it was large, very large by Kevin and Sadie's standards. It was Georgian, said the man, who added, by the way, that his name was Mr Sullivan.

"Sadie and Kevin McCoy," said Sadie. "And Brendan and Tamsin!"

Mr Sullivan showed them all over the house, opening the door of every room and cupboard, showing them every last little pantry. He was obviously delighted with his new possession and pleased to have someone to show it too.

"It's beautiful," said Sadie. "Dear but it's lucky you are!"

"I know that," said Mr Sullivan.

And then he had to drive back to Birmingham. They stood in the roadway waving him off.

"Nice man," said Kevin. "I've a feeling he's had to work hard to get where he is." He wasn't afraid of hard work himself, only wanted the chance of it.

"Wouldn't it be great to have something like that?" said Sadie, looking back towards the house.

"I wouldn't be for saying no if it was forced upon us!"

They spent the night in the village, parked beside the pub. Whilst Sadie was giving Brendan his tea Kevin went for another walk, taking a different road out of the village. It was narrow and winding, cut into the hillside and had an aspect of leading to nothing very much, apart from a farm perhaps.

About a mile along he came to the first signs of habitation, but one which had been abandoned a long time ago. Set back from the road stood the ruins of a cottage, once sturdily built of Welsh stone and slate, but now virtually roofless and windowless, with weeds sprouting through the floor and the remains of old birds' nests hanging from the chimneys. He went inside. He could imagine living in a cottage like this, though not in such a state of course! He grinned at the thought of Sadie up to her ankles in weeds. But a big fire going, the windows and doors replaced, a good tight roof overhead, and how snug they could be! From the windows you would look out on to the range of hills. There was no other habitation in sight though there must be a farm somewhere around the corner. Yes, it would be fine . . . He shook himself. Such dreams to be having! You would need money to do all those things, a lot. And they had none.

He stood in the doorway. It was darkening outside, the sun was dropping behind the hills, which had turned a dark purple. It was a wild lonely piece of country this, much wilder than Cheshire, which, in comparison seemed placid and settled. He had only just set foot in Wales, yet could feel already that it was a country more brooding and changeable than the one they had left that morning. Something here appealed to him, made his senses quicken. It was less predictable—that was it! He had always felt that in Cheshire he could see how everything was at one fell sweep. Yes, he liked this place, could live here. Could Sadie? It would scarcely matter if she could or not: it was unlikely to be for them.

In the evening, when Brendan was sleeping, they went into the pub and sat talking to Mr Hughes and some of the locals. By the time she settled down in her bunk that night Sadie felt as if she knew the business of most of the village. That was the way of small places, a way she had come to like. At first she had hated it, but in fact it wasn't much different from her street back in Belfast. They had lived in a very tight circle there, knowing everyone, everyone knowing them. It had its drawbacks, of course, but it did have advantages: you were never lonely, always had someone to talk to.

The morning was bright and clear again.

"Sure isn't this the loveliest van you ever did see?" said Sadie, as she stood before it. It looked a bit like an ice-cream van, but she didn't mind one bit. She thought of Linda Mullet in her red car and didn't envy her at all, not at all.

"Sure, wasn't Linda Mullet the end?"

But Kevin had forgotten all about Linda Mullet; his mind was on Wales, and the coast in particular. They had a splendid ride, passing through steep-sided valleys, going over mountain passes, watching the peaks of the Snowdonia range change and re-form, and coming at last to the beautiful coast of Merionethshire, lapped by clear blue sea. They found a place that Mr Hughes had recommended called Shell Island, which was not a proper island, being joined to the mainland by a strip of land. As soon as Sadie and Kevin reached it they knew that it was here they wanted to spend their holiday.

It was the first week in September. The sun shone almost continuously, the sand was warm, as was the water. They spent half of the day in the sea, and Brendan and Tamsin loved rolling in the white frothy waves. They bought Brendan a spade. Digging came to him naturally and he worked with great energy, flinging sand in every direction.

In the evenings they sat on the beach, drank beer and coca-cola and watched the moon come up. It was one of the most fantastic weeks she had ever spent, said Sadie, as she lay in her bunk looking out through the window at the faint glimmer of the sea, listening to its rustle and splash as it hit the shore. She wished they might never have to go back to civilisation, to thoughts of work and houses.

Every day Kevin thought lazily that he should go to a phone box and ring Mr Maxton to find out if there was any mail for him. It had been his intention to check in daily but, since coming here, he had found that he was not all that bothered. He knew that he would have to do it sooner or later and had been content to let it stand that way. For these few days he hadn't wanted to know what mail there was, fearing there might be another letter from County Tyrone with red printed letters on the front marked URGENT. His mother had done that to him before. When he had ripped it open, he had discovered that one of the younger children had had to go into hospital to have her tonsils out. That was enough for his mother to send for him urgently. She seemed to have changed out of all recognition from the person she had been when he was small, when she had coped with everything. Of course she had lost his father, and lost him tragically. How did he expect her to be over that in two or three years? It might be something she would never recover from, and then, too, there had been his Uncle Albert half blown to bits and now a hopeless invalid on his wife's hands. There was always a lot to remember.

"Wouldn't it be a great giggle if me ma had arrived when we were away?" said Sadie. "Linda Mullet said she was in a mind to come over again." Miles away, surrounded by sea and sand, she could afford to be amused by the idea.

"She wouldn't come without writing though," said Kevin.

If anyone was to come without writing, it would be *his* mother. He shuddered when he thought of the prospect but no, surely not, of course not, she would never come, make the journey across the Irish Sea unaided. And Brede would see to it that she did not.

The next day, when they went into the nearest village to shop, Kevin decided that the moment had come to telephone Mr Maxton. It was something that could no longer be avoided. Their week was almost up. And perhaps, who knows, there might be a letter waiting offering him a job?

Sadie stayed in the van with Brendan and Tamsin. She sat up in her seat watching him through the phone box window.

Kevin waited for the phone to be lifted at the other end. It was Mrs Maxton who answered. He asked if there was any post for them.

Yes, there was, said Mrs Maxton, but there was something else too. She was very glad that Kevin had phoned for they had been wanting to get in touch with him. Kevin felt a lurch in his heart. Had something happened to his mother? But no, it was not that. What then?

"Your sister's here, Kevin. She arrived two days ago looking for you."

Chapter Seven

KEVIN turned to look out through the glass at the red and cream bus, at Sadie sitting in the front half-turned towards Brendan behind her. He could see the boy's brown arms waving and Tamsin's nose pressed against the window. And in Cheshire, his sister awaited him.

"Are you still there, Kevin?"

"Yes, I am, Mrs Maxton." He said that they would be back the next day to see to Clodagh and he'd be very grateful indeed if they could give her a bed for one more night. Mrs Maxton said that would be no trouble.

He put down the receiver, pushed open the door.

"Well?" demanded Sadie, leaning out of the van window. He looked blank for a moment, so she added, "Any letters? Offers of jobs? Big fat cheques?"

He had forgotten, with the other news hitting him, to ask where the letters were from.

Sadie shook her head. "The sun's really got to you, hasn't it?"

"I said we'd be back tomorrow. We can collect our post then."

He climbed up into the driver's seat and drove them back to Shell Island. Lying on the beach, he wondered how to tell Sadie about Clodagh. She'd blow her top. She'd had Gerald last year. Wasn't that enough? He'd only gone back to Ireland a few weeks ago. Kevin decided he would tell Sadie in the evening when Brendan was asleep, but when evening came another young couple joined them and they sat till midnight. By the time he got into the bus afterwards, Sadie was asleep.

Brendan was awake early, demanding food, wanting out. Out! He wanted to be out all the time. Sadie gave him a biscuit and deposited him on the sand, then began to cook breakfast. Kevin lay watching her.

"Sadie," he began.

"Uhuh?" She turned to look at him, smiling, her green eyes wide open, full of trust and happiness. Little tendrils of damp fair hair clung to her forehead.

He could not get the words out. He said, "We'll come back here again, shall we?"

"You bet! Bacon's nearly ready. Are you for getting up?"

They sat at the table in the van and ate breakfast, Tamsin waiting hopefully under Brendan's feet. This was the best area for titbits: and the dog knew it. Already the bus was beginning to feel like a home. Small though it was, it had everything they needed, said Sadie. Kevin wondered how it would take another person, a full-grown girl? It was out of the question to have Clodagh in here with them, of course it was. But what were they to do with her?

He would send her back to Tyrone, firmly. And he would take no arguments from her. She was under age, and could have the law after her if she did not go.

Sadie enjoyed the drive back to Ellersley Hall, Kevin scarcely saw the mountains and valleys this time. Just outside the village, he drew up at the side of the road. "I've got something to tell you, Sadie." Abruptly, he told her, then sat back and waited for the storm. For a moment she was quiet, stunned almost, then she exploded. He got the lot: his mother, the Roman Catholic church, the nine children.

"Dear, but you've a nerve expecting me to take on that lot, Kevin McCoy!"

"It's not the lot. One. And I'm not asking you to take her on. I'm only saying she's there."

"I know what that means! Didn't we have Gerald for months?"

"That was different."

"I hope so! It'll need to be."

Brendon, sensing trouble, began to cry, which made Sadie calm down. She picked him up and cuddled him on her knee telling him everything was all right. No more was said of Clodagh. Sadie returned Brendan to the back seat, which he did not fancy much, then they drove the rest of the way to the Maxton's house.

When Kevin pulled up outside, Mrs Maxton opened the door at once and came down the path.

"Your sister's in the garden, Kevin. Round the back."

Sadie stayed with Mrs Maxton, the child and the dog; Kevin went to his sister.

Clodagh lay stretched out on the grass, her arms behind her head, her eyes closed against the sun. She was a tall girl with short dark hair. She might have been any girl at all. Kevin hardly recognised her. Or knew her.

"Clodagh!"

She sat up, shading the sun from her eyes. "Oh, is it you, Kevin?" she said casually, as if she had seen him but ten minutes before. She got to her feet, came across to him.

He saw now that her eyes were very dark, black almost, as they were with most of the McCoy children. If he had not known it, he would have thought that she was more than fifteen years old. She wore jeans and a shirt, but they looked expensive and not as if they had been bought from the local store near their home in Tyrone. He stood for a moment studying her. He felt quite inadequate to cope with the situation, was tempted to call for Sadie, but knew that he must not.

"I think you and I need to have a wee talk. Let's go for a walk."

"If you like." She seemed undaunted, unbothered even.

They set out across the fields, Kevin walking fairly fast and Clodagh keeping up with him easily. She had long, slim legs; she was much taller than Brede, the one that Kevin had been closest to.

"I think you owe me a bit of an explanation like," he said at last, rather heavily. He felt he had been put into his father's shoes, without ever having wanted to be in them.

Clodagh shrugged. "Got fed up living with that lot. Nothing

but wailing brats! So I just took it into my head to run away."

"But you can't do that."

"I've done it, haven't I?"

"Clodagh, you've a good home. You'll have to go back."

"I've no intentions of going back. So it's a good home I have, is it? You got out of it fast enough."

"That was different. Anyway, I was seventeen, I had no work in Belfast and Father was alive too."

"Aye, well, you try living with our mother now. She'd drive you round the twist. It's only the boys in the family she's time for anyway, you should know that."

Kevin looked at her. He had never known that, never suspected it. "She likes Brede, doesn't she?"

"Oh, I suppose she does right enough. She needs her plenty." Clodagh tossed her head. "I don't know how Brede puts up with her, honest I don't. She never gets a minute's peace. But then, you know Brede."

Yes, Kevin knew Brede, that she was gentle and patient, would never leave home and abandon her family. This girl was quite obviously a different matter. And what was he to do with her?

"I couldn't stand living in the back of beyond either." Clodagh gazed out across the fields. "I like a bit of action."

"I'll need to send a telegram home, to let them know you're all right."

They headed back towards the Maxtons' house, where Sadie, Mrs Maxton, Brendan and Tamsin now sat in the garden. Sadie jumped up as they approached and looked with interest at the slim, dark-haired girl at Kevin's side.

"Sadie, this here is Clodagh. Clodagh, this is Sadie."

Clodagh said, "Hi!"

Sadie said, "Hello, Clodagh."

After that there was silence, broken by Brendan, who came trotting into the middle of their circle crowing at the top of his voice. He stood before Clodagh and looked up at her with a grin. She gazed back down at him, said nothing.

"This is Brendan, Clodagh," said Kevin.

"I thought it would be." She turned away from them, walked to the edge of the garden, where she stood with her back to them. Sadie was riled. She might at least have spoken to the boy, he had been standing in front of her waiting for a word. Sadie felt hurt to have Brendan rejected.

Clodagh took a packet of cigarettes from the pocket of her jeans and lit one. Sadie and Kevin glanced at one another. Kevin shrugged. What should he do? He was not sure. The girl should not be smoking, would be better off not, but did he have the right to tell her what to do? He supposed in a way that he did, since he was her eldest brother, and standing in for his father. But he made no move towards Clodagh.

She turned and came back towards them, smoking her cigarette, unabashed by the stares that followed her. She blew out a long stream of smoke, rested her hand with the cigarette on the angle of her hip and smiled.

Kevin said hastily that he had best be off to the village to send a telegram to his mother. Clodagh said she would come with him, she could do with a change of scene. As soon as they had driven off, Sadie exploded. Mrs Maxton shook her head, sympathising, saying that surely Sadie had enough to bear without having a girl like that shoved upon her.

Sadie sighed. "It isn't Kevin's fault, of course, Mrs Maxton."

She took Brendan and Tamsin and walked up the drive to the big house where she found Mrs Willis and Mrs Jones in the kitchen. They jumped up, pleased to see her, when she poked her head round the back door.

"Can I come in? Is it safe?"

"Of course, come away in, Sadie lass." Mrs Willis went forward to gather up Brendan into her arms.

The kettle was put on, tea made, and cakes brought out of a big tin. Mr Allan had taken up residence, they told Sadie, with his wife and two daughters. What were they like? Did Mrs Willis and Mrs Jones like them? Sadie fired questions at them, eager to know all, to catch up on the gossip. The housekeeper and cook were cautious, they weren't sure yet, they were giving it time, but so far, they were not too thrilled.

"Different class of people altogether," sighed Mrs Jones. "You should see the daughters!"

"And hear them!" added Mrs Willis. "Teenagers. And the cheekiest I've ever had to listen to."

Talking of cheeky girls led Sadie on to Clodagh. They had already met her, and could appreciate Sadie's problem.

"She's not one bit like your Kevin, is she?" said Mrs Willis.

No, she was not, at least not in character, but Sadie had to admit that they did look rather like one another. Didn't they think so themselves? Mrs Jones nodded. The same black eyes, the same tall slim bodies. You would know they were brother and sister all right.

"What are you going to do with her, Sadie?" asked Mrs Jones.

"Dear knows! I can see that one won't be so easy sorted out. You just have to look at her to know it."

Sadie had disliked her on sight, hated her manner, the way she had walked across the garden, the way she had ignored Brendan and looked at them all.

There was a rap on the kitchen door. It opened to admit Kevin.

"I thought I'd find you here, Sadie."

"Come away in, Kevin," said Mrs Willis, "and have yourself a cup of tea."

He was followed in by Clodagh who sat herself down at the end of the table. Sadie noticed that she had another cigarette between her fingers. She leaned back against her chair with one hand dangling over the back, her legs crossed.

"I've sent the Maxtons' phone number," he said to Sadie. "And asked Brede to give us a ring."

They drank their tea and left. Again, Clodagh went with them, back to the Maxtons. Sadie jumped straight into the bus and started to cook their tea. Outside, on the low white wooden fence, Clodagh sat staring at the hedgerow, waiting to be fed. Sadie flipped fish fingers angrily about in her small frying pan, and almost cut herself when she opened a tin of beans.

"I'm sorry, Sadie love," said Kevin softly. "But what can I do at the moment?"

"Nothing, I suppose. But you'll need to get her back on a boat to Ireland as fast as you can or it'll be me that's heading for the hills."

They ate inside the van and afterwards Clodagh got down and stretched herself in the road. She made no offer of help with the dishes, reminding Sadie of the way that Gerald had been when he had first come to them. What was it with the McCoy family that none of them would offer help? Perhaps that wasn't fair, for she knew that Brede would, not only help, but probably take over the running of everything at the same time. She was their martyr. Well, one would do them! They weren't going to add Sadie Jackson to their list.

Around eight o'clock Mr Maxton came to his front door looking for Kevin. A phone call from Ireland.

He dashed into the house, with Sadie behind him. Clodagh had gone for a walk up the road. It was Brede on the line, as Kevin had expected; she spoke in the same soft gentle voice, saying that she was glad Clodagh was safe. They had been worrying about her night and day. She was a wild one right enough, and their mother couldn't cope with her. Neither could Brede herself, she had to admit; none of them knew what to do with her.

"I'm afraid she can't stay here with us, Brede," said Kevin. "As a matter of fact I've lost my job and the house that went with it. We're living in a van at the moment."

"Oh dear!" Brede was sorry, for them in their troubles and also, well, they had been hoping that perhaps they might have been able to keep Clodagh with them, for after all, hadn't they worked miracles with Gerald?

For a moment Kevin felt anger. What did his family think he was? Some form of care and protection society for their delinquents? Then he calmed. They must have enough on their plates over there, were glad enough to get rid of one problem.

Brede said that their mother was there wanting to have a word with him. She sounded strange, his mother, coming across the line over the Irish Sea. Her voice was faint and weak, and she said what he knew she would say, "Why don't you just come home, son? Sure you'd like it fine once you were here and Mr Burke could let you have a cottage."

"Blackmail!" hissed Sadie, who had been standing close enough to hear what was going on. She turned and left the room, unable to stand any more of it.

"Look, Ma, I'll have to send Clodagh back. I'll have to, I tell you. We have no house—"

"But I'm at my wits' end with her, Kevin. Surely to God you could keep her for a wee bit? It isn't much I'm asking of you, is it?"

It was a lot, Kevin wanted to shout, but if he was to shout she would start to cry. Patiently, he said again that they had no house, nowhere for her to sleep. Nowhere. Where were they sleeping then? asked his mother. When he told her she said, "Couldn't you just let her have one of the bunks in the van?"

Kevin groaned. They had been brought up in a small, cramped house, a house the same size as Sadie's, but there had been many more of them and they had been used to sleeping three and even four in a bed. He knew, without having to ask, that Sadie would not go for it. And why should she? She deserved better than that.

The pips went again. "We'll need to go," said his mother. "We have no more money."

"Wait!" cried Kevin.

But she would not wait, she said goodbye, and may God look to him, and the receiver went down. The line was dead. He rattled the receiver rest but she was beyond his reach. And they were not on the phone in their cottage so he had no way of contacting them, except by writing or sending telegrams. And letters and telegrams could easily be ignored.

She can't do this to me, he thought, she can't! She is being unreasonable, quite unreasonable. This woman had changed out of all recognition to him. And this woman was his mother. He wanted to choke.

He thanked the Maxtons, went back to Sadie. She sat in the van, Clodagh sat on the fence in front of the garden. He could not ask the Maxtons to give Clodagh a bed for another night, they had done enough.

"Sadie—"

"She isn't sleeping in here with me, she's not, I can tell you that right now. If you let her come in here I'll sleep in the field and I'll take Brendan with me."

"I'll sleep in the field," said Clodagh, who had overheard the conversation through the open window. "I don't mind."

"No, I'm sure you wouldn't," said Sadie. "I dare say you're not fussy where you sleep."

Clodagh did not rise to the jibe. She gave her little cat-like smile and continued to gaze out across the fields.

"You can't sleep in the field, Clodagh," said Kevin.

"Why not? I've done it before."

Kevin wound up the windows of the bus. "I can't let her sleep out in the fields, Sadie. She is my sister, and she's only fifteen."

"And *I* am your wife. And I'm only twenty."

Kevin wanted to say that he was only twenty-one and look what he had to cope with! He didn't know how to cope either, didn't know how to begin to break such a deadlock. He knew full well how stubborn Sadie could be, and from his short acquaintanceship with his teenage sister saw similar determination in her. Neither of them were the type to bend, as Brede would have done, to make some suggestion to smooth everything over. He longed for Brede to be here amongst them as a ministering angel.

He got out of the van and went for a walk up the road. The evening smelt good! Scents of warm grass and blackberries. Whenever he had troubles on his mind he always walked; the movement of his legs seemed to help the movement of his mind. His mother was trying to push the responsibility of Clodagh on to him, but he was unwilling to take it. It was not really a case of being unwilling: he could not because of Sadie. Tomorrow he would take Clodagh to Liverpool and put her on the Belfast boat; he would warn her that he was notifying the police that she was returning, that she was a minor who had run away from home.

But what of tonight? That had to be got through first. The evening was dying, the sun lowering into the land, suffusing the Welsh hills in the distance with bright pink and orange. Those hills beckoned to him, suggesting a haven of peace. He longed to go back there.

He turned, still unresolved as to what to do for tonight. Coming towards him, he saw Clodagh.

"You don't have to worry about me," she said. "I've told you, I

74

can kip anywhere. An old barn'll do."

"I can't let you—"

"Oh, don't be so stuffy. I remember when you were fifteen you were as wild as get out. Now you're a stuffy ould married man. In those days you were never at home and Ma was never done worrying about you."

It stopped him in his tracks, thinking back to those days, for it was true that he had been wild, and so had Sadie. To Clodagh they must seem like a very settled-down married couple. But it still did not mean that he could allow Clodagh to sleep in the fields, or in a barn.

Mrs Maxton was standing at her gate, leaning her arms over the top of it. She called out to him, and he left Clodagh to go to her. She said that she thought it would be best if Clodagh slept with them again that night.

"Are you sure you don't mind?" said Kevin gratefully. "It'll just be for the night. I'm taking her to Liverpool tomorrow and sending her home."

Chapter Eight

IN the morning, they awoke to find that Clodagh had flown. The Maxtons had not heard her go; she must have slipped away in the dead of night, tiptoed down the path, past the red and cream van in which her brother and his wife slept, and carried on up the road. To where? She had taken all her clothes with her in the one suitcase that she had brought.

"It was quite a dear suitcase too, real leather," said Mrs Maxton, adding, "She had her real leather jacket with her as well."

"Where would Clodagh have got money to buy a jacket and case like that?" Kevin asked Sadie, when they were alone.

Sadie shrugged. "From a man maybe? Unless she nicked it."

Kevin did not much fancy either explanation, but he knew full well that Clodagh would have not got the money from her mother to buy such expensive things, nor could she have earned it either. He put that question aside to face the more important one. Where had she gone? Where was she now?

They had to go to the police, to report her missing: there was nothing else for it. Driving into Chester, having dropped Sadie, Brendan and Tamsin off in the village, Kevin kept his eyes roving from one side of the road to the other, hoping that he might see the girl sitting on her suitcase. But there was not a trace of her.

The police said that it was nothing new, a fifteen year old girl missing, there were dozens of them everywhere. They quoted figures. How had she got over here from Ireland in the first place? they wanted to know. Where had she got the money from? Kevin did not know, he had not got around to asking her the evening before, though it was doubtful if she would have told him if he had. The police were a little more interested in this case, because she was Irish. Kevin sighed inside himself, knowing that this was only to be expected. Sometimes he felt that you had only to be Irish to be suspect, for anything. Clodagh would not be mixed up in anything political, he said. Did he know for certain? He had to shrug at that, for he did not really know Clodagh. He felt that he knew nothing for certain any more, if he ever had. They said they'd keep an eye open, do all the usual things, let him know if they came up with anything, but from the way they spoke, it was obvious that they didn't expect to find her. Of course they couldn't put the police force out to look for headstrong fifteen year old girls bent on running away, Kevin knew that, and did not expect it.

On his way home he stopped at all the petrol stations, taking detours, trying all the roads in the area. No attendant could remember seeing any girl that answered Clodagh's description.

Probably gone to London, one policeman had said; that's where they usually make for, think it'll be the answer to all their dreams. Nightmares more likely! And once they disappeared into the huge city, it was like trying to find the old needle in the haystack.

Kevin found Sadie sitting in Mrs Hughes's kitchen, drinking coffee by the fire. She had gone to the village to see the doctor (she was as fit as a fiddle, he told her) and called in at the pub afterwards. She and Mrs Hughes were not talking of Clodagh, but of Mr Hughes's brother who had slipped and broken his leg the night before and had been taken to hospital. Mr Hughes was getting ready now to drive over and visit him.

"It's a terrible business," said Mrs Hughes, shaking her head. "Poor Tom! And him all alone with no one to help him in the pub."

"Kevin," said Sadie, who looked as if she was about to burst with excitement, "I was just saying to Mrs Hughes that we could go and help out at the pub until Mr Hughes gets back on his feet again."

"Well, I don't know," said Kevin hesitantly. He could hardly think about it.

"Sure it would be dead easy. Nothing to do but pour out beer and chat to the customers. It would be something to tide us over until you get another job, Kevin."

Mrs Hughes told Sadie to give Kevin time to think; she poured him a cup of coffee and sat him down by the fire. She said he looked dazed, which wasn't at all surprising, considering all the troubles he had on his back.

Kevin scratched his head. Already Sadie was about three miles ahead of him, making for Wales, and *The Speckled Hen*. He had Clodagh on his mind. He said that they couldn't go anywhere without her, they would have to wait until she was found.

"If they find her they can send her on," said Sadie.

"Send her on?" said Kevin. "You try sending that one anywhere."

"What's the point of hanging around waiting for her? You might wait months."

Kevin pulled Brendan up on to his knee and sat looking into the fire over the boy's head.

"Sure I know you're dead worried about Clodagh," said Sadie. She herself, she had to admit, was not; more than that, she was delighted that Clodagh had taken herself off and hoped that she would never show her face to them again. It might be a terrible unchristian thing to be thinking but that was how it was. She was sick of Kevin's family, wanted to escape them, to go over the border into Wales. "At least let Mr Hughes speak to his brother about it."

Kevin agreed, if only to have a quiet life. He had enough raging around in his head at the moment, without having to argue with Sadie. Working in a pub? That wouldn't bother him any. He was prepared to do anything that would keep body and soul alive. It would only be temporary of course. Again! He was sick of everything being temporary, wanted something permanent, wanted roots. Roots. That to him still meant Ireland, and he could not escape from that.

They spent the day in the vicinity of the Maxtons' cottage, in case there would be any word of Clodagh from the police. There were men working with bull-dozers in the fields, flattening everything in front of them, tearing up trees, destroying the farm that Kevin had loved. He wished, too, that they were miles away, over some border and out of reach. But he could not escape from the fact that Clodagh was his sister, and only fifteen years old.

Sadie took a long time to fall asleep that night, knowing that Kevin was wide awake and likely to remain so until dawn. She could just make out his arms folded behind his head, and sensed that he lay with his eyes wide open.

Mr Hughes came along early in the morning to say that his brother was interested in having Kevin to stand in for him for a while since he didn't much like the idea of shutting up the pub. It was the only one in the village.

"What do you say then, Kevin lad?"

"Yes. I made up my mind during the night. I'll take it on, we need the money and I hate being on the dole. Can't stand it." He said that they would go the following day, he wanted to stay here one more day in case Clodagh would turn up. If she did not appear by then he thought that she would have gone far away and her chances of coming back would be slender.

Sadie was delighted. They would be able to live in the pub, in a proper house again, instead of being bunched up in the van.

"Only for a few weeks," Kevin reminded her.

But you never knew, did you, they might be able to stay longer, Mr Hughes might decide he wanted help all the time? Kevin warned her not to think that way, it was unlikely, Mr Hughes was not a rich man and the pub and village were small to support a publican plus another family.

"It's a stop-gap," he said. "A breather."

"The story of our life," said Sadie jokingly.

Kevin worked in the Hughes's pub that day, to get his hand in, as it were. Mrs Hughes said that she thought he would do very well indeed, and Sadie was just the right person to make everyone feel at home. Sadie did her washing and ironing in Mrs Maxton's kitchen, scrubbed out the van from one end to the other, ready to take off on their new life.

As they were settling down for the night, they heard a car approaching. Headlights lit up the van. The car stopped, the engine died. Kevin sat bolt upright, immediately sensing that it might be news of Clodagh. Sadie lay back, fervently hoping that it would not be.

There was a rap on the window, a voice—unmistakably a police voice—saying, "Are you there, Mr McCoy?"

Hastily Kevin pulled on his clothes, stepped out into the cool evening. It was a police car that had pulled in behind theirs, and huddled in the back seat was Clodagh.

"We found her when we picked up a man in a stolen car."

"I'm sure that she would have had nothing to do with it," said Kevin quickly.

"So she said. She said she'd just been hitching a lift so we've decided to let her go. She's all yours!"

Chapter Nine

THE journey into Wales was not the joyful trip that Sadie had anticipated. She sat staring straight in front of her, trying to ignore Clodagh who lounged silently in the back of the van. She had been silent ever since the police had deposited her on Kevin, having merely shrugged when Kevin asked her to account for herself. He had decided to leave it then, to question her no further, but to try to have a good long talk with her when they got up to the village. From time to time Sadie's nose twitched as she smelled the cigarette smoke. At last, unable to contain herself any further, she turned round.

"Would you mind putting out your cigarette, Clodagh? It's making me feel sick and it isn't good for the boy."

Without a word, Clodagh tossed the glowing cigarette end out of the window. Then she settled back in a corner with her eyes closed. She looked as if she hadn't slept for a night; her hair was tousled, her face none too clean, her jeans grubby.

By the time they reached *The Speckled Hen*, Clodagh was asleep. They let her stay there and went inside. The woman who cleaned for Mr Hughes was waiting to show them where everything was, and where they were to sleep.

Inside the pub Sadie could forget Clodagh. Once more she was excited, by this new turn in their lives. All right, even if it *was* only temporary! She was not going to get too carried away by it all, she promised Kevin; he shouldn't worry so much.

"But you can't help it, can you?" he said softly, putting his arm round her.

Sadie aired the beds which had not been used for a long time and swept out the upstairs rooms. It looked as if Mr Hughes had shut them up when his wife died.

As she went down into the bar to help Kevin, Clodagh appeared, yawning, rubbing her eyes. She looked around with interest.

"Not a bad pub," she said. "Seen worse in my day."

"Well, you won't be seeing anything of this one," snapped Sadie. "You're under age and you'll stay out of here."

Clodagh raised an eyebrow, sauntered around, hands in the pockets of her jeans, eyeing the copper pans on the wall. She was wearing the expensive leather jacket. For a moment Sadie wanted to demand where had she got it, but held back, knowing that Kevin would think it was his place to ask such questions.

There was no time for him to ask any questions that day. They had a rush to get ready for opening time, not that they were exactly knocked down by customers trying to get in, but they wanted to be ready and waiting when anyone did appear. One or two old men came in quite early and settled by the log fire, and then, gradually the place half filled. It was seldom more than half full, Mr Hughes had told them, except on a Saturday night. Then they often got visitors from outside, week-enders, even day visitors.

Sadie put Brendan to bed in one of the little attic rooms and came down to help Kevin in the bar. She got to know quite a number of the customers that evening.

About half an hour before closing a young couple came in making Sadie's head turn. The girl was very pretty with long brown hair hanging to her waist and she wore a long flowered dress with a shawl about her shoulders; the young man had long hair and a beard and strings of beads around his neck. Obviously not natives!

"Hello." The girl had a sweet smile. "You related to Mr

Hughes?"

"No," said Sadie, and proceeded to give them the run down on their lives, hers and Kevin's, and explain how they had come to be here. They appeared interested, listened and nodded sympathetically. They knew what it was like to be hard up, always trying to make ends meet. They went on to tell Sadie that they were potters and trying to make a go of running their own business. They had bought an old cottage with outhouses where they had built a kiln.

"We're just about to go into production," he said.

"That's great!" said Sadie, impressed.

"But we don't know yet if we'll sell anything," said the girl.

"I'm sure you will," said Sadie with confidence. "I really think that's marvellous. At least you've got something of your own to do, to take a chance on. Now Kevin and me—" She stopped, shrugged.

"You must come and see our place," said the girl. Their cottage was a mile from the village.

"I'd love to."

The girl was called Angelica, the boy Matthew.

"Angelica and Matthew," said Sadie dreamily, as she and Kevin were rinsing out the glasses after closing. "Romantic names, aren't they? I thought they looked dead romantic. Angelica might not be a bad name for our new baby, Kevin?"

Kevin tipped out an ashtray into the bucket. "Angelica McCoy? Can you imagine it?"

"Well, maybe not. But she was pretty, wasn't she?"

"Didn't notice."

"Oh, you!"

Clodagh did not appear at any time during the evening.

Next morning, after they had cleared up the place from the night before, Kevin sought his sister out. "Come for a walk, Clodagh."

She got up and went with him. They did not speak until they were quite a way outside the village. It was a fine autumn day, with leaves, burnt orange, ochre yellow and cinnamon brown crunching under their feet. They listened to the noise of the leaves.

Eventually Kevin spoke.

"We can't go on like this." He did not know quite what else to say, how to put it, what to ask her. She was beyond his range, even though she was his sister. "Will you not go home, Clodagh? At least till you're sixteen and then you can leave and no one will bother you."

He stopped, appalled by what he had said, for it implied that nobody would be interested in her fate after she was sixteen years of age. She scuffed the road with her feet, stirring a knot of leaves. She did not want to go home, she did not have to repeat it. They walked on again.

"Where did you sleep the night before last?"

"In a field."

And that was all: she would offer nothing more than the minimum answer every time. He asked about the man in the stolen car but she said, as the police had done, that she had hitched a lift and that was all, she had known nothing about the man. Was that true or not? Kevin could not decide. He could not decide if he could trust her word or not. Most of his experience with her, in the short time since she had come over to England, had shown that he should not trust her. He said that she could not stay with him and Sadie, she could not expect to.

"O.K., so I'll go."

He sighed. "Why did you run off from the Maxtons?"

"I heard you saying you were going to put me on the Belfast boat. You couldn't expect me just to sit there waiting, could you?"

He did not know what he could expect, except further trouble. When they returned, Sadie looked at him immediately with a question in her face. What had he done? What had he arranged with Clodagh? Nothing, he told her, he hadn't been able to get through to her, not at all. Then she would just have to try, said Sadie; if he had failed it was only fair for her to have a go. He conceded.

Sadie went upstairs to Clodagh's room. The door was ajar. She entered with a quick knock saying, "I want to talk to you, Clodagh."

Clodagh half lifted her head and looked somewhere around

Sadie's knees. Sadie sat down and said with determination, "I want you to listen to me." Then she tried to tell the girl how awkward and difficult their lives were, how big a responsibility Kevin had to bear, and that his sister had no right to come here worrying him still further. It was her duty to return to her mother and family in Tyrone.

Clodagh lifted her head, looked Sadie levelly in the eye. "I'm not going back, and you can't make me, can you? Not unless you tie a rope around my neck and drag me, like a cow."

Sadie cried out, "You're a selfish little—" She stopped. It was like banging your head against a brick wall. She stormed down the stairs to demand that Kevin *do* something.

"But I don't know what to do, Sadie," he said helplessly. "The only way I could get rid of her would be to take her on the boat myself back to my mother. And even then could you see me, man-handling her down the gang-plank?"

Sadie's rage subsided, and she grinned.

"If I tell her to go she probably would, but can I do that?" asked Kevin. "Send her off God knows where?"

The trouble with him was that he had too strong a sense of family responsibility, said Sadie, sitting down to cool off. It was just as well he did have, was it not, he asked, for after all he was collecting quite a family himself to be responsible for?

"Aye, you're a good man, Kevin McCoy, even though me ma wouldn't admit it! By the way, did I tell you I had a letter from her before we left the Maxtons' yesterday?"

She went to fetch the letter and read it aloud. Her mother had written to tell her that she was the unhappiest woman alive, that Linda Mullet had just returned from her honeymoon bringing the news of Sadie's terrible disgrace. Sadie looked up at Kevin. "What do you think of that then? And get this: 'You'll be the death of me yet, Sadie Jackson. I've told you before and I'll tell you again, you've brought terrible shame on our street and on this house. Linda Mullet has been swaggering up and down ever since she came back in her fancy shoes and her fancy coats. She says you're going to live in an ice cream van.'" Sadie laughed, folded the letter. "Me ma and I'll never understand one another."

"No more will me and mine," said Kevin, with a grin. "Looks like we just have to live with that."

Sadie could well imagine the scene, with her mother moaning and groaning, clutching her arms about her chest, rollers all over her head, and her father sitting behind the paper, rustling it and grunting every now and then. What did we ever do to deserve it? And then, Mrs Mullet would be rapping at the door from time to time, to borrow two eggs or a quarter pound of tea and asking, "And how's Sadie then? Any news, Mrs Jackson?" Ever since Linda had made such a good match her mother would have been smiling from her door step as if she was waiting to see Royalty itself pass by any second.

"So what do you want me to do then, Sadie love?"

"Oh, let her stay for two or three days while we think it over. Maybe we'll have a brilliant idea or something'll turn up."

So Kevin told Clodagh that she could stay for a few days, on condition that she helped in the house, did some of the cleaning and didn't get too much in Sadie's way. Clodagh did not say whether she accepted the conditions or not. But she did help in the house, was a hard worker when she started, scrubbing floors and making a good job of them, for she'd been brought up since she was a small child to do chores. She also chopped wood in the back yard and worked in the garden. Her arms were strong. In the evenings, when they were in the bar downstairs, she sat upstairs in her room, doing they knew not what. And Sadie did not care as long as she remained there, not getting into any trouble. The two girls only communicated with one another about things that were essential, like passing the salt or who was going to do the washing up. For the first time in her life Sadie had come across someone she did not want to talk to. Even with Gerald it had been different in the beginning; she had wanted to get through to him, to try to provoke him into some kind of response, but with Clodagh she felt as if she were facing a closed door. Locked and barred.

"I suppose she should really be at school," said Kevin.

Sadie looked at Kevin with astonishment; she could not imagine Clodagh at school, sitting in history classes, doing maths, coming back with homework! It didn't seem one bit likely that they could ever persuade her to go near a school so they dropped the subject. After all, they reasoned, no one here would know what age Clodagh was for she looked at least two years older than she was and would not be on the authority's records.

Within a few days Sadie and Kevin were well known in the village and the surrounding area. Sadie took Brendan and Tamsin and went to call on Angelica and Matthew who had just fired their first batch of pots and were in a mood for celebration. They opened a bottle of home-made wine. Elderflower. Sadie sipped it cautiously, deciding that it was very nice. Angelica and Matthew made their own wine, jam and wholemeal bread, bottled fruit, kept hens and grew vegetables. They were trying to be self-sufficient, they explained, and also to live only on real food. Nothing canned or adulterated for them.

"You should bring your boy up only on the good things of the earth," said Matthew, lifting Brendan on to his knee. Brendan settled down contentedly to play with Matthew's strings of beads.

Sadie had never thought very much about the kind of food they had. She supposed it would be a good idea but knew herself well enough to realise that she'd run out of something before too long and have to resort to the tin opener and a can of beans. It sounded as if you would have to be terribly organised.

"It's worth the trouble though," said Angelica.

Sadie adored their cottage and when she went home told Kevin all about it and that he must come to see for himself. The walls were white inside, the curtains woven (by hand, by a friend of Angelica's), the floors covered with rush mats. There were flowers growing inside and out, and a wood fire had blazed in the grate. Sadie had come home as dusk was drawing in feeling slightly drunk from the wine, the woodsmoke and the new ideas swirling around in her head.

"It was really heavenly, Kev."

Kevin went with her next time, and he, too, liked the cottage. Who could not?

"They're like us really, aren't they?" said Sadie, as they walked back along the road into the village. "I mean, getting by on next to nothing. They haven't a penny to spare either."

That was true, Kevin admitted, but he did not think their situations were all that alike.

"Why not?"

"Well, they'll never starve, will they? They've both got a good education at the back of them and their families have money. Matthew told me his father had paid for the cottage."

"Do you mean you feel they're sort of playing at living simply? They don't have to?"

"A bit."

"But you do like them, don't you?"

Oh yes, Kevin said, he did indeed. Sadie enjoyed their company and found Angelica refreshing compared with Kitty whose mind ran only on the next piece of furniture or gadget she was saving for. That used to depress Sadie who had no hopes of saving for gadgets. Other than potato peelers! But now Angelica was teaching her to crochet, and with her help she was making a shawl.

"Are you going to be a shawlie then?" said Kevin. Shawlies were what the poor women in Ireland were called, those who were wrapped about with black shawls.

"But a very elegant shawlie!" The shawl was fir green, and Angelica had given her a piece of material almost the same colour (woven also by her friend), which would make a long skirt. Sadie was going to keep it for after the birth of the baby. "And Angelica's going to teach me to bake bread. What are you grinning about?"

"Nothing. Nothing!"

This life suited her, Sadie decided: the days were well filled. And the evenings, although seldom very busy, brought a few people to nurse a pint of beer beside the open fire, and since they were not run off their feet there was time for her to have a bit of a crack with them. She got to know how many children the different farm workers had, what their wives were like, and sometimes on a Saturday night they brought their wives with them. There were not many young people, apart from Angelica and Matthew, the teenagers tended to go away to the towns, so the population seemed to be either middle-aged, elderly or very young.

"We could be doing with more of your age group, Sadie," said

Mr Wright, the minister. Sometimes he came in at lunch-time, to have a quiet half pint and smoke his pipe. The church and manse were opposite.

"Dear knows if we'll be staying," said Sadie. "When Mr Hughes gets back I expect we'll have to move on. We're always doing that. Moving on."

Mr Wright was full of sympathy, wished he could help, but could think of nothing going in the district that would suit Kevin. There were complications with the fracture of Mr Hughes's leg so he had been taken into a convalescent hospital and there he would remain for three or four weeks. It was bad for Mr Hughes but good for them, because it gave them a bit of a respite. Sadie did not allow herself to think beyond that.

Kevin did though, could not but help it. When Mr Hughes comes back it would be mid-October, and then November would be coming in fast, with its damp, dark afternoons, not quite the time of year to be sleeping in a van with no insulation. He didn't want Brendan to start getting a cough, and for Sadie herself to feel cramped in a van. During the times when the pub was closed, Kevin walked a lot, across the fields and into the hills. He loved the countryside, especially the hills, which were not high here but were peaceful and had a feeling of remoteness. He wouldn't even mind being a shepherd on these hills but he smiled, thinking of Sadie, knowing that she could not be a shepherd's wife. No one to talk to but sheep!

He walked often too along the narrow road that led past the ruined cottage. He always stopped. The house had had four rooms: the partition walls were still partly standing. Two bedrooms, sitting room, living-kitchen. And the bathroom? That would have to be built on at the back, as a lean-to. The last cottagers no doubt had done without such a refinement. Probably without running water and electricity too. In his head he built up the cottage, dug and planted the garden, replaced the broken fence. Sadie could strew the floors with rush mats if she wished. That would be all right by him!

It belonged to the nearest farm: that he soon discovered. The farmer came upon Kevin when he was sitting on one of the broken window sills. Kevin jumped up apologising. He did not mean to be trespassing.

The farmer did not mind. The old place was far gone now, he said, lighting his pipe, pushing his hat back on his head; no one could do much harm to it.

"Pity," said Kevin.

"Aye."

"Would you ever think of selling?"

But who would ever think of buying? demanded the farmer. It'd cost a pretty penny to put that back in shape. His only chance of a sale would be if some monied folk from the Midlands wanted a week-end place.

The farmer wished Kevin good day and they parted.

Returning home, Kevin found Mr Sullivan in the bar. Sadie had newly opened up.

"Do you remember Mr Sullivan, Kevin?"

"'Deed I do." Kevin and Mr Sullivan shook hands.

Mr Sullivan said that they had just got possession of the house and estate and were hoping to move in in a couple of weeks. He had come back to have another look, to gloat over his new property! Sadie cooked him some supper since he was sleeping alone in the big house that night. It was seldom that they did meals, although Sadie did not mind from time to time, and whenever strangers came in saying that they could find nowhere to eat, she was happy to oblige.

"Not very fancy, I'm afraid," she said "but it'll fill a gap."

It was just grand, he informed her, and he enjoyed his meal very much. He was grateful to her for taking the trouble for sure she must be busy enough as it was. She was only too glad to be busy, she informed him, since it meant having a roof over their heads.

He sighed. "Aye, life can be difficult. *I* know all about that."

"You do?"

"Certainly. There've been times when I didn't know where the next meal was coming from."

"You see," Sadie said to Kevin later, "Mr Sullivan came up from nothing and now look at him with that grand house!"

Kevin smiled. "You think the same fate might be in store for us?"

"Well . . . You never know though, do you?"

Kevin agreed that you never did, although he had a feeling he didn't have Mr Sullivan's flair for business.

They were quite busy in the bar that evening and so neither of them had time to notice where Clodagh was. When Sadie had put Brendan down to sleep, she had noticed that the door of the girl's room was shut. After closing up for the night, rinsing the glasses and dousing the lights, they went upstairs.

Kevin called out, "Goodnight, Clodagh."

There was no answer, but often she did not answer when spoken to.

"Are you wanting any supper?" asked Sadie, feeling a little guilty for sparing so little time for the girl.

Sadie and Kevin looked at one another, and the same thought came into their heads. Somehow, they both knew that she was not there. Kevin opened the door, confirming their suspicions. The room was dark and empty.

"She hasn't gone for good," said Sadie, spying her leather suit-case. "She must just have gone out for the evening."

"I wish she'd told us," said Kevin. "And where could she have gone to round here? It's not exactly Piccadilly Circus."

They went to their bedroom, though Kevin did not undress. He sat on the edge of the bed. Sadie, tired, got inside and lay down. She said that he was daft to wait up for her, she could take care of herself and would return, in her own good time. Kevin knew that that was true, but, nevertheless, could not but feel anxious under-neath.

"She's only fifteen after all."

"I wish you'd stop saying that," snapped Sadie. "You're like a gramophone record. She might only be fifteen but she's been around all right!"

What did she mean by that? Kevin wanted to know. There was no call for Sadie to cast aspersions on his sister's character, without knowing anything for certain.

"For dear sake! Can't you see with your own eyes what she's like? Nothing but a tramp." Sadie turned over in bed pulling the sheet over her head. She was sick, fed up with Clodagh.

Kevin was silent. He continued to sit on the edge of the bed. Sadie kept the sheet covering her eyes. In the end, exhausted, she drifted off into an uneasy sleep.

At midnight Kevin went out and took a turn up and down the road. There was nothing to see but darkness, not even a moon to-night, no stars either. At one o'clock, when he was sitting down-stairs by the window, he heard a car come roaring up the village street and screech to a halt outside.

He opened the door to see Clodagh emerging from the car. The car was one he recognised, belonging to one of the farm hands from a farm further down the valley. The boy himself was about twenty years old and a bit of a tearaway, so it was said, driving too fast, drinking too much, and generally annoying everyone. He seemed a likely character for Clodagh to have picked up.

She came sauntering up the path towards her brother. "See you, Cliff," she called back over her shoulder. Cliff roared off, Clodagh and Kevin went inside.

"Now don't start," said Clodagh.

"I've every right—"

Clodagh yawned. "Oh, I know you think you have every right but spare us, can't you?"

Why should he? he demanded. She didn't spare them anything, and then this evening she had gone off leaving him to worry about her. He didn't have to worry, she told him, he could have gone to his bed, knowing that she would come back. So why had he bothered?

She made to go up the stairs; he caught her by the wrist and pulled her back down, quite fiercely. "Now listen here, Clodagh McCoy. If you're going to live under my roof, you'd better do as I say."

She laughed. "Dear, but you sound like our da used to do. I remember him ranting at you and Gerald many's the time. Not Brede. She never did anything to annoy anyone. Little saint that she is!"

For a moment Kevin wanted to strike her, and was appalled that he should feel this way towards his sister. He let go of her, turning away, feeling once more that this was something he could not cope with.

"Why did you bother coming to me at all, Clodagh?"

She did not answer for a moment, then said, "Well, you're my brother, aren't you?"

"Does that mean anything to you? After all, you have a mother back home, and that doesn't seem to mean much to you."

"It doesn't mean much to her, you mean. She doesn't bother her head over me so why should I over her?"

"Oh, come now—"

"Come nothing! She doesn't, Kevin. She has too many others." Clodagh shrugged, took a battered packet of cigarettes from her pocket and lit one. "It's not much fun being one of nine, *you* should know that."

They sat down, Clodagh unbuttoned her coat. Yes, Kevin admitted, he did know that, and being the eldest was probably the least fun of all, but they should not blame their mother for that.

"She didn't have to have nine kids, did she?"

Maybe not, but she had had them, and there was no use thinking about it any other way.

"When I was a kid I used to think you were great." Kevin, startled, glanced at her and she added, "I did, honest. You didn't notice me much, you hadn't time. I used to think you were the tops. I suppose that's why I came."

"I remember you turning cartwheels in the street," said Kevin, with a smile.

They talked, of their old home in Belfast, of their mother and father and brothers and sisters. It was a long time since Kevin had thought about them all in detail, had recalled memories of a time that seemed to be so far back in his past that it was almost as if it had happened to another person. He and Gerald had never talked like this, even though in the end they had got on quite well together. Clodagh remembered all sorts of things about him, things that he had done when he was fifteen and sixteen, and she was a small girl. There were moments when they even found themselves laughing.

In the middle of it, Sadie burst into the room.

"What in the name are you two doing down here at this time of the morning? It's three o'clock and nobody can get a wink of sleep for the noise that you're making." Then she flounced back up the stairs in her bare feet, her hair swirling angrily around her shoulders.

"I don't think anything I could do would please your wife," said Clodagh. "She doesn't like me, does she? Don't bother answering, Kev, I wouldn't want you to be telling any lies for my sake."

Clodagh got up and walked up the stairs to bed, leaving Kevin with his thoughts.

Chapter Ten

"O.K., so she's not as hard as she looks. She's just a sweet little girl underneath. I've got the message, thank you very much."

"Try to like her, Sadie," begged Kevin. "You're usually so good with people, I'm sure you could get through even to Clodagh in the end."

Sadie was not sure that she wanted to try. The girl disturbed her in many ways. For one, and this was not one she particularly liked to dwell on, she felt a bit jealous of her, because she took up so much of Kevin's attention. It was stupid to feel jealous, but she did.

Clodagh started to go out regularly with Cliff in his car, coming back late at night, even though Kevin continually asked her to come home at a more reasonable time. She said she would try, but never made it. She said that she forgot once she was out. In a way Kevin understood that for he had been just the same when he was her age, not that he had gone out in fast cars, but he used to roam the streets till after dark, returning much later than his father had liked. He had been very restless at that stage in his life, had hated to come back to the tiny little terraced house, to the bedroom that he shared with his other brothers, where you could hardly swing a mouse, let alone a cat. At least Clodagh had a bedroom to herself and they were not crowded on top of one another, not at the moment anyway. But Mr Hughes would not stay away for ever.

Mrs Owen, who kept the Post Office and General Store, confided to Sadie that Clodagh was the talk of the district. "She's a real wild one that," she declared, as she wrapped up a lump of cheddar and laid it on the counter with a smack. She leaned closer to Sadie. "I hear she's often to be seen in Ruthven, in the pubs!" She nodded, pursing her lips.

It did not surprise Sadie to hear it, nor did she doubt that it would be true.

"And she must be under age, is she not?"

"She's not sixteen yet," said Sadie, and then could have bitten her tongue out for she and Kevin had decided that they would not let anyone know Clodagh's age. But she had been carried away by her desire to have sympathy from Mrs Owen and the need to talk to somebody about Clodagh and the trial that she was to them. As the days went by Clodagh and Kevin were getting on better and better: they talked and laughed, and often Sadie felt excluded. Kevin said that she was daft to feel that, and she should be glad he was getting on a bit better with his sister. She grudgingly said that she was, of course.

"Isn't that terrible?" tutted Mrs Owen. "You've enough on your hands, Sadie, without having the likes of that. After all, you've your own wee lad to think of and another coming."

Sadie went to talk Clodagh over with Angelica and Matthew. They thought that Clodagh was misunderstood.

"Whose fault is that then?" demanded Sadie.

Not Clodagh's necessarily, they said. She obviously felt she had to wear protective armour. They thought that her life had been under-privileged.

"I wouldn't say mine has been over-privileged."

But she had great inner resources, they said.

"Do I?" asked Sadie, astonished.

They thought that what Clodagh needed was love.

Sadie held out her glass to be refilled with rhubarb wine, feeling in need of something to bolster her strength to cope with the idea of trying to love Clodagh. It was the only way she would ever succeed in making any kind of connection with the girl, said Angelica and Matthew.

After a day of trying—or sort of trying for she found it difficult to know how to begin—Sadie decided that she was not saintly enough to love Clodagh. In fact, she had to admit to herself that she *detested* her, not that she would ever dare confess it to Angelica and Matthew who seemed to hate no one, not even Angelica's mother who kept writing nasty letters threatening to cut her daughter out of her will if she did not face up to the responsibilities of life.

"Poor mother," was all Angelica said, and committed the paper to the log fire flames, whilst Matthew lit another stick of incense.

One day, Sadie hoped, she herself might cultivate such serenity. But in the meantime . . .

And then, Mr Hughes came home. He said that he could use their help for another couple of weeks, but after that, well, he would have to ask them to go, for he could not afford to have them stay. They understood that, knowing that he made only enough to live on from the pub himself and he would not want three other adults, a small child and a dog for company, not for long.

Two weeks, thought Kevin. And then what? Hostages to fortune. The words ran in his mind again like a mocking jingle. The village doctor had booked Sadie in at the local hospital, but would they even be in the district then?

He began to buy magazines and newspapers, to search the *Situations Vacant* columns. He felt little inclined to move away from here, to go off to Herefordshire or Somerset, places that he had never seen and knew nothing of. Neither of them wanted to move to yet another strange area. They were beginning to know this one and to be known themselves.

Sadie left Kevin studying a farming magazine and took Brendan and Tamsin for a walk in the woods, which were shedding leaves in every direction. They were drifting down on them even as they walked.

On her return, she found that Kevin had a visitor: an official from the local education authority. Someone had reported Clodagh for not attending school.

"It must have been Mrs Owen," said Sadie with fury afterwards. "When I lay my hands on her—"

Kevin reminded her that it could have been one of another half dozen people, for surely Mrs Owen would have passed the word around, since everybody enjoyed adding on their own little bit about Clodagh as the stories went from mouth to mouth. It did not matter too much who had reported them. The upshot of it was that Clodagh was to be sent to school!

"You've got to be joking!" she declared, when she heard. "Me at school?"

She would have to go, Kevin told her, or he would be up in court. So Clodagh, after a lot of protesting, slamming doors and finally sulking, went off to school. The school bus came round every morning gathering pupils, stopping at the farms, and then finally in the village.

"Never thought I'd see the day!" said Sadie, as she watched Clodagh climb aboard. "That's a real turn up for the book. Maybe it'll do her good."

Kevin reminded her that she had not been too keen on school herself, had done her share of complaining, and even mitching.

Within a week Kevin had a note from the headmaster asking to see him. He went, with a good idea why he would have been summoned.

Clodagh was insolent, obstinate, and completely impossible, he was told. The teachers could do nothing with her, she would do nothing for them: it was a stalemate. Kevin shrugged, saying that he was sorry but he couldn't do much about her either, he was only her brother and she was a difficult girl.

"Can she not go home to Ireland? She needs a father to look after her."

Kevin explained about his father and the headmaster was sympathetic, sighed, and said they would try again. One week later Kevin was asked to go back again. This time he was told that Clodagh had not been at school any day in the previous week. She had set off from home in the morning, catching the school bus, but she had never got as far as the school gates. The other pupils, when questioned, said that she jumped off the bus before they reached the school and disappeared.

"I'll have a word with her," said Kevin heavily. Though what good would a word do?

It was time too for them to be moving out of the pub: their two weeks were up, although Mr Hughes had never mentioned it again. Sadie wondered if they need go if he didn't mention it, but Kevin said that that would not be fair, for he could not continue to keep them, give them free accommodation, when he did not need their services any more. So, that evening, Kevin told Mr Hughes that they would be moving out in two days' time.

"Aye well," said Mr Hughes, "I could really only do with someone in the evenings now, from about seven o'clock onwards. So if you're staying in the area, Kevin, you could still lend me a hand then."

Kevin accepted, for part-time work was better than none, and there was always a chance that he might be able to do a few hours' gardening. There were a number of elderly, retired people, who'd built bungalows in the district and were incapable of heavy digging themselves. Mr Hughes looked unhappy when he saw the McCoys packing but they tried to make him feel that it was not his problem or his fault they were going to live in a van again. But they knew that for the last week they had, in fact, been getting on the older man's nerves, that Brendan made too much noise, that the dog barked too often, and on top of that, Mr Hughes could not be doing with Clodagh. She annoyed him, the way she talked, the way she smoked, and the way she came home late at night, disturbing the household. Kevin recognised that it was time he moved his bunch out.

"Some bunch we are too!" he said. He looked round at his wife, son, sister, dog. And soon there would be either a second son or a daughter.

They parked the bus just outside the village on a small piece of land in front of a wood; it was a lovely spot with a view out over the hills. Neither Sadie nor Kevin would have minded too much, even though the weather was quite cool and crisp, if it had not been for Clodagh. It was such a small space in which to live with someone who was so difficult. The first night hardly any of them slept at all, apart from Brendan, who slept peacefully and obliviously. Sadie tossed and turned and remarked how stuffy it was, and overhead, in the upraised roof, Clodagh lay silent on her bunk. It was cold up there, in the roof space, at this time of year.

The next day, she came back to say she had found herself a room in a cottage belonging to an elderly widow, who was willing to let her have it for nothing in return for some help in the house. Sadie went to see Mrs Roberts. She was one of the few people in the village that Sadie had never met and when she did, understood why. Mrs Roberts was badly crippled with arthritis, could scarcely hobble, and was also quite deaf. She and Sadie shouted at one another for a few minutes and at the end of it Sadie was not at all sure that Mrs Roberts had gathered who she, Sadie, was, and what her relationship was to Clodagh.

But Mrs Roberts did say that she was a God-fearing woman, she kept a good house, and would take on the girl. She had told Clodagh apparently that there was to be no nonsense, no young men brought into the house, or coming in late, or anything of that sort. Sadie did not doubt that Clodagh had sat and listened and agreed to nothing: that was her way. She never disputed terms or rules; she simply went her own way.

Sadie went back to report to Kevin. She thought they had no alternative but to let Clodagh go. So Clodagh packed up her few belongings in the expensive leather suitcase. They never had found out where she had got it from, though Sadie had asked her, unable to resist it. Clodagh had shrugged. She had picked it up somewhere, couldn't remember where. She implied that it was of no interest whatsoever.

It was a relief to have the van to themselves again, and with one person less, as Sadie declared, it even seemed quite spacious. It would serve them well enough for a few days or even weeks, but once the baby came, what then?

Chapter Eleven

NOVEMBER arrived dank and wet.

"Typical," said Sadie aloud, to herself, as she stared out at the dripping trees and the mist that hung like skeins of wet wool across the hills. Visibility was virtually nil, and she hated not to be able to see as far as she wanted: it made her feel closed in. She felt even more closed in because Brendan had a cold and had to be kept inside.

What a funny life it was to be leading! If her ma could have seen her she'd have had a purple fit! Sadie grinned and almost wished that her mother would come tottering down the road. The van would upset her more than the two seedy rooms they'd had in Liverpool. Tinkers! *Sadie Jackson, I never thought I'd live to see the day . . .*

Brendan and Tamsin were both sleeping. Sadie got up and went out for a few minutes, to stretch herself to her limits. At times she felt so cramped up in the van that she was desperate for a bit of space to move in. The baby inside her was growing large and beginning to tire her. She had thought about it little so far, but now was beginning to.

Kevin had found two or three gardening jobs, and every evening he helped Mr Hughes. He drove the van up the pub, parking it there with Sadie, Brendan and Tamsin inside, not liking to leave them alone by the wood in the dark. Sadie was glad enough to see *The Speckled Hen*'s lights through the window, to hear footsteps and voices coming and going. Evenings were her most difficult time for the light in the van was not bright, could not be, otherwise Brendan would not have slept. She could not see well enough to crochet or read, so she sat half listening to the radio and the wind rustling in the trees, half dozing, thinking. Occasionally Angelica came and sat with her but she and Matthew were very busy glazing and preparing pots for the Christmas market. They had got in some orders; things were beginning to move for them.

Clodagh never came to visit them though Sadie knew that Kevin saw her. She glimpsed them sometimes in the distance together, walking and talking. You could tell they were talking, from the way they held their heads and the way they turned to one another every few seconds. Angelica and Matthew told her she should be pleased. She tried to be. When she questioned Kevin he said that Clodagh did not really tell him much about what she was actually doing and he did not ask her. What did they talk about then? This and that. He was vague. Their family. Home. *Home?* repeated Sadie. He said she should not be so jumpy: it was only a manner of speaking, and the only home he had now was with her and Brendan. Some home it was! she declared.

One day, she had two visitors: the Sullivans. They were passing, out for a walk, and Mr Sullivan wanted Sadie to meet his wife. Sadie invited them in.

"Not much room, I'm afraid," she laughed. "But I think I could squeeze you in."

"Not living in this thing, are you?" asked Mrs Sullivan in her soft Welsh voice.

"It's not too bad, you get used to it."

"But that's dreadful, isn't it, Patrick?"

Mr Sullivan agreed. He looked about, frowning, saying that surely it must be possible for them to do better than this. They'd done worse before, in a way, said Sadie, and described to them the two rooms in Liverpool. She saw them looking at one another and had an uneasy feeling that she knew what they were thinking. *Look at us in our big house, just the two of us . . .*

"But I really love the van," she said hurriedly. "Honestly! It's just great. It's real snug so it is . . ." She gabbled on singing its praises as if her one ambition in life had been to inhabit such a vehicle. Then she seized the kettle and made them coffee. The subject was changed: to the gossip of the village, a matter on which Sadie could offer much information.

The Sullivans went away, came back next day. They came to offer the McCoys accommodation in their house.

Sadie's face flamed. "Did you think I was hinting yesterday—?"

"Indeed we did not," said Mr Sullivan emphatically. "But when we got home we started thinking."

"And we thought that here were we in this great big house and there were you—"

"But you've worked for your big house," Sadie burst in.

"That's neither here nor there," continued Mrs Sullivan. "The fact of the matter is that we have more space than we can possibly use and you have much much less than you need."

"But—"

"Now listen, Sadie. We've talked it all out, Patrick and I, and we know there could be difficulties on both sides, but with a bit of patience there's no reason why it shouldn't work. We could give you some rooms and perhaps in return you could give me a hand in the house when you're able?"

"Of course!"

"And perhaps Kevin could give my husband a hand? We'd work out some financial arrangement too, depending on how much Kevin would do, so that it'd be fair all round."

Then Mr Sullivan said, "I'm thinking of buying a couple of cows and my wife wants to keep hens. We're going to have a big garden full of vegetables and try to be as self-sufficient as possible."

"Kevin would love to help with all those things," cried Sadie. "Sure he's a whiz with the cows and the hens and all. He's got green fingers. He's really a farmer at heart, you know, even though he was brought up in Belfast."

They waited till Kevin returned from his gardening job. He, too, seemed stunned to begin with. The Sullivans were actually offering them a home?

"That's right," said Sadie happily. "Isn't it marvellous, Kev?"

He nodded; that was all he seemed to be able to do.

"I don't know if I can employ you full-time, Kevin," said Mr Sullivan. "Though perhaps indeed it might come to that, when I get the cows, and we start trying to till the land, eh? Do you know, it's always been a dream of mine to have a bit of land and live off it? It's an Irishman's dream, isn't it, lad? I've lived all my life in the city but now I'd like to have a go at this. It'd certainly be better for me to have someone like you to help me."

He suggested that Sadie and Kevin should come along the following day to the house and have a look at the rooms, and discuss arrangements.

When the Sullivans had gone, Sadie and Kevin sat quietly for a moment, then Sadie said, "Seems a bit like a dream, doesn't it?"

"It does that."

"Aren't you pleased then? You're just sitting there not saying very much."

Of course he was pleased, there was no question about that. What was the matter then? Well, he shrugged, the only thing that bothered him was that they always seemed to be dependent on the charity of others, they never seemed to be able to rule their own lives. They had to go where fate took them, where the tide tossed them up, as it were, and they were at the mercy of other people's whims, or deaths.

"Oh, come on now, Kevin, you shouldn't be thinking that way. I'm just glad to have somewhere to be going to at the moment. The future'll have to take care of itself. Sure haven't we always known that?"

Kevin smiled at her, took her hands in his. "You're a marvellous girl, Sadie. I think you could cope with anything. It's dead lucky I am to be having you for a wife."

Her eyes twinkled. "Is that right now? I'm glad to hear you say it."

"You know it!"

"It's another adventure, Brendan," she told the baby, as she pushed him along the road in his push-chair the next morning and up the drive to the big house.

Mrs Sullivan was waiting; she had been making plans.

"She loves to have something to organise," said Mr Sullivan.

Sadie and Kevin's rooms were to be on the ground floor at the back: the servants' quarters. Sadie did not mind that one bit, had not expected to inhabit the grander rooms. They were to have three, next to the kitchen. That would give them a sitting room and a bedroom for themselves and the other one, a very little room would do for Brendan, and eventually the baby.

"It's fantastic," said Sadie. "It's awfully kind of you."

"Nothing of the sort," said Mrs Sullivan briskly. "After all, it's not just a one way thing, you'll help us as well."

Sadie prayed fervently inside herself that it would work, that they wouldn't get on the Sullivans' nerves too much. She would well understand if they did, especially since the Sullivans were getting on a bit in years, and they, the McCoys, were not the quietest outfit around. She resolved to try and move about the house as silently as she could, for she had a habit of clattering things a great deal, dropping pot lids and the like, and singing and whistling to herself. The dog and the baby would be less easily quietened. But Mrs Sullivan looked a different kettle of fish from Mrs Ellersley: she was plump and motherly looking, and she smiled at Brendan and talked to him.

"I don't see why you shouldn't move in straight away," said Mr Sullivan, who had come into the kitchen behind them. He stood in the doorway puffing his pipe, smiling kindly.

There was nothing at all to prevent them: it was not as if they had to wait for a furniture truck or anything like that. Kevin simply drove their cream and red van up the road and along the drive and round to the back door of the Sullivan house. Within minutes they had moved their few possessions into the house. The three rooms were already furnished so Mrs Sullivan said there was no need to send for their own stuff from Cheshire, it would cost a lot to transport and wouldn't be worth it.

In spite of Mrs Sullivan's protests, Sadie insisted on starting to help in the house. She was as strong as a horse, she informed the older woman, and enjoyed having something to do. So she dusted, washed dishes, and kept the kitchen clean and neat. She liked to feel that she was earning their board.

Mr Sullivan and Kevin too got straight down to the business of buying cows and hens. They went to the market in Mold together and purchased three fine *Fresians*.

"They're grand beasts," said Mr Sullivan. "Great sight, eh Kevin lad?"

Mrs Sullivan got her hens too, helped by Sadie, who had picked up a bit about the care of fowls whilst at Ellersley Hall. Kevin started also to turn over the land in preparation for planting. The man who lived in the gatehouse looked after the parkland, cutting the grass and keeping the trees clipped, but there were a number of jobs for Kevin to do. Mr Sullivan paid him a reasonable amount, though not as much as Kevin had earned as cowman at Ellersley Hall, so, in addition, he kept on his job at the pub, for Mr Hughes's leg was taking a while to mend and he was unable to be on his feet for long.

"I'll stay with Mr Hughes as long as I can," said Kevin. "We're going to start and save a bit, Sadie, for I've decided that we must buy our own house."

"Us? Buy a house? You're joking!"

"Probably only a small cottage, maybe even half derelict, but I could build it up myself. Wouldn't that be great? And then we'd be our own masters."

Indeed it would, if it could ever come off, but money was difficult to live on these days, let alone to save, and when you did put any by what was it worth in the end? Everyone said there was no point in saving now. Even Angelica and Matthew, who did not usually say what everyone was saying.

"Well, we're going to," said Kevin with determination. "I'm opening an account with a Building Society and I'm going to put away my pub money every week. We've still got the ten pounds the Ellersley Hall folk gave us. That'll be our first deposit."

Sadie wished that she could earn something, as she had done before, but of course she didn't get any pay from Mrs Sullivan, did not expect it. She worked for their rent, and they got their electricity and heating thrown in. It meant they could live on Kevin's pay from Mr Sullivan and save the pub money. There was no question of her taking another job elsewhere at the moment, not in her condition at any rate. Even after the baby was born she would have her hands full, said Kevin, so she was to put out of her head any nonsense about jobs. She sat and pondered over the *Situations Vacant* column in the newspaper, reading all the ads on how to make money, but there didn't seem to be anything very much that she could take on, not living here at any rate. This wasn't much of a district to go out selling cosmetics in of an evening! For a couple of weeks she did the football pools, winning nothing. Sitting there filling in the crosses, she thought of her father doing his pools every Thursday evening, come rain, shine, or even bombs. He had seemed to have the knack, had won several times.

Her mother wrote to say that she would like fine to come over and see the new baby after it was born. Sadie wrote back to say that at present they had no room but knew that would not stall her mother for long if she was determined to come. She supposed they could put her up in the sitting room but hated the idea of bringing one more person into the house to bother the Sullivans. Not that the Sullivans seemed to mind; they were an easy going, good-tempered couple, who didn't have jangly nerves or bother too much if Tamsin barked occasionally in the night. Tamsin and Brendan loved the place with the parkland to roam in freely. Sadie loved it too: it was so peaceful, so much what she needed to await her baby in. She was to go into hospital in Ruthven to have it and Mrs Sullivan said that she would manage Brendan fine when Kevin was not about.

"Don't you worry about the little lad," said Mrs Sullivan.

They wrote to the Hughes in Cheshire and told them to get rid of their furniture; they couldn't expect them to keep it indefinitely and it was of little value, things they had picked up for next to nothing in sales. The Hughes wrote back enclosing a cheque for fifty pounds. They had managed to sell it to a young couple who had just got married.

"Fifty pounds!" cried Sadie, waving the cheque. "Not bad."

Kevin took it at once to deposit in the Building Society. Another step towards their new house.

"Listen to your da!" said Sadie to Brendan. "Our own house!"

December was colder but drier. In the mornings the frost lay sparkling on the ground.

"Christmas is coming and the geese are getting fat," sang Sadie to Brendan. "You'll enjoy Christmas this year, boyo."

She and Mrs Sullivan were baking Christmas cakes, puddings and shortbread. The Sullivans had invited them to have Christmas dinner with them.

"Everything's going fine," said Sadie to Kevin, and could have bitten her tongue out later, for next day, Clodagh was evicted. She appeared in the driveway carrying her suitcase.

Chapter Twelve

THEY had to take Clodagh in, there was nothing else to be done. It was not surprising that she had been put out by Mrs Roberts, for inevitably, she had come up against her. It was only a miracle that it hadn't happened earlier. Mrs Roberts had found Cliff in Clodagh's room one evening. He had come in through the window.

"Why on earth do you have to go and do things like that for?" stormed Sadie.

Clodagh sat in Sadie and Kevin's sitting room saying nothing as usual, or as little as she could get away with. She got away with everything, thought Sadie; it might do her good to have a real shock one of these days. She had had plenty in her time, Kevin reminded her, what with the death of their father and all the troubles in Belfast and their mother going half round the bend.

"O.K., O.K.! I know it all. You don't have to repeat it."

Sadie felt cross and irritable now, and the lovely time they had planned to have at Christmas seemed threatened. Kevin had to go and ask the Sullivans if they would mind if Clodagh stayed with them for a while, until they found her some other accommodation. The Sullivans, who had not taken to the girl any more than anyone else did, were not particularly enthusiastic, but they did not refuse.

"You'll have to behave yourself, Clodagh," Kevin told her

sternly. "You're not going to get us put out of here and all."

Sadie doubted if Clodagh would pay any attention but she did come home earlier than she had done before, and stayed out of the Sullivans' way, seldom going into the kitchen. She had to sleep on the settee in their sitting room which did not please Sadie very much, for every morning, getting up, she was faced first thing with the sight of this girl huddled in sleep.

"I don't know what we ever did to deserve it."

It had seemed enough to have had Gerald, but she knew very well that it was because they had had him that they now had Clodagh. One had followed the other in a kind of logical sequence. Who would it be next?

"Who's next in line?" she asked Kevin. "Who's the next youngest, I mean?"

Kevin frowned: he had to think. "Kathleen, I think."

Sadie nodded. "She'll be the next one to get sent over, you can bet your boots on that."

"Don't talk daft!"

"Sure why don't they all come at once and let's get it over with?"

Kevin said no more. There was no point in arguing with Sadie when she was in such a mood. Besides, at the moment, with the baby soon due, he did not want to argue with her at all.

They draped the house with streamers and lanterns, tinsel and mistletoe. Kevin and Mr Sullivan cut down a fir tree which they set up in the hall, and Sadie and Mrs Sullivan decorated it. It was a beautiful tree and every time Sadie went into the hall it made her catch her breath.

On the morning of Christmas Eve, they had yet another arrival. He came in the early morning, knocking at the back door. Kevin went to see who it was.

"Gerald!"

"Hi, Kevin! Can I come in?"

"I suppose you'd better," said Kevin, leading him into the kitchen and through the hall into the living room. He pulled back the curtains to let in the daylight. Clodagh rubbed her eyes and sat up. "Is it you, Gerald?"

"Aye, it is."

He was carrying a holdall, and he looked as if he had been awake all night, as indeed he had. He had been travelling.

"Well, well," said Kevin, not knowing what else to say, not knowing what he would say to Sadie. He took a cup of tea through to her in the bedroom. She was lying awake, with her arms behind her head. She smiled at Kevin as he came in saying that it was Christmas Eve and this was going to be the loveliest Christmas they'd ever had.

Kevin sat down on the side of the bed and let her drink her tea before he broke the news. She sat bolt upright, knocking the remains of the tea across the eiderdown.

"Take it easy now, Sadie love. You mustn't get yourself worked up—"

"Worked up? Do you blame me?"

Kevin said that Gerald had only come to spend Christmas with them. He was returning to his job in Ireland afterwards. Sadie calmed down and said, "Oh well, I don't mind him coming for a day or two. As long as it is no more." Their little part of the house was bursting at the seams already, and she was afraid that Mrs Sullivan might not be crazy about housing any more McCoys.

But when she went into the living room, she was pleased to see Gerald again. He even gave her a kiss!

"Sure you're looking great, Gerald. The work must be suiting you."

It was, said Gerald, he liked the stable rightly, and the owner was good to him. They sat and chatted and caught up with their news. And it was not long either before Brendan was back on Gerald's knee.

Alone, in the kitchen, Sadie sang, "I'm dreaming of a McCoy Christmas." Now that she had got used to the idea she was going to make the best of it. In fact, it might not be half bad to have a bit of a family party. If only Clodagh would make an effort, smile a bit more and try to be nice! She went around with that grim hard look on her face all the time which didn't make you feel much like having her company. Kevin said that she was of a different temperament to Sadie, and Sadie should keep that in her mind when trying to deal with her. She must not expect Clodagh to be like herself.

It was a busy day, and by evening Sadie was dead tired and ready to lie on the settee and put her feet up. Brendan went to bed, unaware that Christmas Day was almost upon him. His mother informed him that when he awoke in the morning there would be lots and lots of presents which Santa Claus would have put there during the night. He was more interested in the ear of a blue bunny rabbit.

Kevin came into the room as she was putting out the light. "Shush!" she said, silencing Kevin. "I think he's about to topple over."

They went out into the corridor where Kevin told Sadie, rather abruptly, that he, Gerald and Clodagh would be going to Midnight Mass. They always did on Christmas Eve, even Clodagh who did not go to church very often now.

"You didn't go last year."

"No, I couldn't. There wasn't a church nearby and I didn't want to leave you."

"But you'll leave me this year?"

"Ach, Sadie, be reasonable!"

"Reasonable is it? You go to mass and confession every week, never miss. Well, hardly ever. So why do you have to go out tonight—of all nights?"

"Because it is tonight. It's special."

"For me too. Or am I not important?"

"You know you are."

"But you'll put your church first?"

"You know it's not like that."

"Do I?"

"Dear, but you're pig-headed at times!" He turned away.

She went to the kitchen. He followed.

"I'll stay with you, Sadie, if you want me to."

"But you don't want to, do you?" She put some pot lids on the shelf clattering them noisily. "So what would be the point?"

"I am offering, am I not?"

"Oh, away on to your church with your brother and sister and never mind me!"

She marched in front of him to the sitting room to find that Clodagh was sprawled on the settee reading a magazine. Sadie sat herself down in an armchair and picked up another magazine, but her eyes were too hot and tired to read. She did not look near Kevin.

Clodagh went out for a little while later on but came back in time to go with her brothers. There was no Catholic church in the village, they would have to go to Ruthven.

"Will you be all right, Sadie?" Kevin looked troubled as he bent over her. "I can stay."

She yawned. "I've told you—I don't want you to stay. I wouldn't want to get between you and your church."

The Sullivans were going to mass too, for they also were Catholics. Mrs Sullivan had been a Protestant when she married Mr Sullivan but had changed. She had said to Sadie that she had gone to the church a few times, liked it, so had thought, why not? They had had children, who were now grown up, and it had been easier for them all to go to the same church. Sadie knew that she could never ever 'turn', as she called it. She had been born a Protestant, and would remain one.

They all drove off in the Sullivans' car, leaving Sadie alone with Brendan and Tamsin in the large house. For the first time she was conscious how large the house was, how many empty rooms stood standing silent, and how far they were even from the road. The drive was a long one and winding; it took at least five minutes to cover it, walking fast. But what would she be wanting to walk down the drive fast for at this time of night? She shook her head and told herself not to be such a daft eejit!

Before, she had been sleepy, dozing off and on throughout the evening; now she was restless and fully awake. She could not face going to bed alone, before Kevin returned. She thought she heard a noise somewhere in the house. She got up and opened the sitting room door, stood listening. It must be something moving in the wind, there would be no one else around. Strangers did not come into these parts very often, except in summer.

She went to the kitchen to make herself a cup of hot chocolate. The wind was beginning to howl outside and little flakes of white swirled against the window. It looked as if they might have a white Christmas after all. She drank the chocolate leaning against the draining board, watching the snow drift down. She remembered watching snow drift down when they had first moved into the cottage in Cheshire and how lonely she had felt. Usually she was not lonely here, but tonight she was.

It was only one night, but it was Christmas Eve after all. She supposed that in County Tyrone the rest of the McCoys would be at mass too, Mrs McCoy and the remaining children, Brede and Robert, and Robert's mother and father. Catholics to the last man they were. She was the only one in the whole family who was not.

She was left out. That was the plain truth of it. And no one liked to be left out. She didn't have to be, she could hear Mrs Sullivan telling her in her lilting Welsh voice: she had the choice. Sadie accepted that and chose once more to stay as she was. She knew there was never any question of Kevin making a choice, that he would not even consider becoming a Protestant. And she knew, too, that in times to come Brendan would be going off to church with his father, and then this new baby. She had always known it, but had thought about it as little as possible.

Restless, she wandered along the corridor to the hall where the big tree shimmered with tinsel and fairy lights. It was so beautiful! And it was real. When she was a child they had had a nasty artificial affair which had been taken out of its box, dusted off, and after Christmas packed away again for next year.

Looking up, she noticed that the fairy had slipped from her perch on the topmost branch and was tilted downward looking as if the slightest ripple of a draught might send her plummeting to the floor. That would never do! Sadie fetched the steps from the kitchen and set them in front of the tree, panting with the effort of moving them. They were heavy, she was handicapped.

She took a deep breath, put a foot on the bottom rung. Kevin would have been furious if he could have seen her but then he could not. He was far, far away. At mass. In the Catholic church. With his brother and sister. And she was alone. And would have to rescue the fairy herself.

Slowly, cautiously, she mounted the creaking steps. Dear but she was a terrible weight, she told herself, as she heard them sigh beneath her. But it would not be long now before she would get rid of the weight, not long at all. January was close. Soon she would be glad to be able to move freely again, to run, and jump. She imagined herself running across the parkland, arms outstretched, hair flowing back, and the breeze against her cheek.

Two rungs from the top she paused. She felt a trifle dizzy, even unreal, as she gazed out over the spreading dark green branches of the fir tree and at the little lights winking and glistening, red, yellow and blue. She blinked. One more step and she would be able to reach the fairy. Her head cleared. She made the step.

The fairy's leg was caught inside a branch. Reaching out, Sadie eased the golden-haired doll away from the clutches of the snatching pine, taking care not to snag the white tulle dress. Who would want a Christmas fairy with a torn frock? It would spoil the perfection of the tree.

And then, in the next instant, she lost her balance. She swayed, crying out to Kevin who was not there but who was at Midnight Mass in the Catholic church with his brother and sister, trying to right herself, to regain her foothold; but unable to, fell, bringing the tall Christmas tree and little fairy crashing down to the ground with her.

Chapter Thirteen

SADIE gave birth to a stillborn child on Christmas morning. A son.

"You'll have lots more children, Mrs McCoy," said the doctor. "You're healthy. And you're young. Very young."

She felt very old as she lay in the hospital bed neatly tucked in, not moving, not wanting to. She was alone in a small room. And everywhere, there were flowers. From the Sullivans, Angelica and Matthew, people in the village.

Kevin had been here earlier, with Mrs Sullivan. They had come with her in the ambulance after they had returned from Midnight Mass to find her lying on the floor entwined in the Christmas tree. Mercifully, the fairy lights had smashed and gone out: otherwise the tree might have caught fire. It could have been worse. So everyone told her. It was fortunate also that she had not struck her head, said the doctor. Instinctively she had put out her arms to save herself, catching hold of the branches and thereby cushioning her fall a little. But not enough to save the baby.

For more than an hour she had lain with her leg twisted under her. She had felt quite calm except for moments of panic when she had thought she might die and no one would come or that Kevin would never return and she would lie until spring. Tamsin, hearing the noise, had come running and stayed beside her licking her face from time to time, whimpering, but not barking. And Brendan had not wakened. That, at least, had been a blessing.

Hearing a step in the doorway, she turned her head, saw Kevin. He looked tired, haggard, unshaven. He came to her bed, sat down on the chair beside it. He took hold of her hands.

"Sadie, love, I'm sorry. Terrible sorry. It was my fault! I shouldn't have left you."

"No! It was my fault, Kevin. *I'm* sorry. I shouldn't have climbed the steps."

"If I had been there you wouldn't have done it."

"But I knew—"

What? That she would fall? She had sensed the danger with every step she had taken. She had known she should have backed down. Why had she not? It had been almost a return of the devil-may-care attitude from her childhood. She had always been a one for dares, could never say no, especially to herself.

"You took a chance," said Kevin. "You weren't to know."

"It was stupid," she cried out. "Very, very stupid."

He stroked her hair, hushing her. He said that he had been selfish, he knew that now: he should have put her first.

"But it was special for you to go," she whispered.

"You were special for me to stay."

It was so stupid: that was all she could think. And wasteful.

Her baby was dead.

"Oh, Kevin!" She clung to him, tears streaming.

They could say no more about it that day; neither could speak of it or sort out the thoughts in their heads. When Sadie was calm they talked of Brendan and the house and Kevin asked if he should let Sadie's mother know.

"I suppose." She lay back against the pillow. She was exhausted.

She slept off and on throughout Christmas day. Somewhere, further along the passage, there was the sound of music and laughter and the clink of dishes. They were having a party, the nurse told her. She was not interested.

But when night came she could not sleep. The flowers had been taken out, the room was in shadow. She lay listening to the near silence of the hospital. She lay thinking also.

It had been ridiculous to climb a pair of steps to rescue a fairy, to put her baby at risk. But she knew why she had done it. She had been seething with resentment because Kevin had gone to mass. So many people in the world were seething with resentment over something, boiling over with it, achieving no other end but wastefulness. Kevin's father dead. His Uncle Albert legless. Thousands of others killed, maimed, devastated. What she had done to their child—hers and Kevin's—was no better. She had lost the baby because of those black feelings she had nourished. Yes, nourished! She admitted it.

She had climbed the steps because Kevin was a Catholic. She hated his religion. Always had. And yet had married him. Did it make sense?

Her head ached. She reached out, took a drink of water from the bedside table. It must make sense somehow since she had married him, was living with him, and loved him. It was the last bit that had carried her through, made her ignore his religion. Yes, that was it! For in spite of all the song and dance, the arguings and bickerings, she had ignored this important fact about Kevin. She had never faced up to it, not properly. Not to what it meant. It had been the external aspects that had occupied them more: the attitudes of their families and neighbours to their mixed marriage, the necessity to go into exile because of it.

'If I'd a penny
Do you know what I would do?
I'd buy a rope
And tie up the Pope
And let King Billy through!'

The childhood jingle ran through her head. She chased it away, thinking how silly it was to remember that now. But no, maybe not, for wasn't that it? It went right back to there, and that was a long way back. How did you change that? Could you?

A soft footfall, and in came the nurse to see if she was all right, needed anything? Sadie shook her head. "Don't lie there fretting now," said the nurse kindly, remaking the sheet, feeling Sadie's brow. "It won't do any good."

At times one had to fret, thought Sadie, but did not say so. She assented meekly, and the nurse departed.

If she was to go on living with Kevin she could not go on hating his religion. It would poison her and their life together. But how did you stop hating?

For a start, by wanting to, she supposed.

She could think no more, could take no more. She slept.

In the Sullivans' house Kevin also lay awake, listening to the striking of the grandfather clock in the hall. When it chimed five he could stay in bed no longer, got up, dressed and went out into the dark snowy morning.

He tramped the road to the village, hands thrust deep into his pockets, collar pulled up against the cutting wind. He needed the sharp cold air to help him to think.

Somehow, he had failed Sadie, although he was not sure exactly in what way. It was not just a matter of having left her alone on Christmas Eve. It had been reasonable enough for him to have gone to the mass, said Mrs Sullivan; she said he should not blame himself, it was an accident that could have happened at any time. That was not quite true, Kevin knew, but true or not, it went beyond that, to the matter of their different religions. Of course he knew that, always had. But it had been in the background, kept there as much as possible, deliberately, by both of them.

Sadie had always boiled up more over his religion than he over hers. It was in her nature to boil up; in his, to retreat into himself, mull things over quietly. But there was something else too: Brendan. She resented that he was to be Catholic. And Kevin admitted to himself that she had a point there for he himself would have resented Brendan being brought up Protestant.

Yes: his religion demanded more of her than her religion did of him. He faced that squarely, knowing that he could not change it. It was not possible for him to change it but he must tell her that he recognised that fact. He must try to be more patient with her, to understand her objections, he must try to talk to her. They had never really *talked* about it.

How strange! And yet it had been at the centre of everything between them.

She looked very pale when he went to see her. And quiet. Quiet for her. A spasm of anxiety puckered through him. But what else could he expect when she had just been through such a terrible experience? The doctor had said that she was in very good condition considering, and he did not expect to keep her long in hospital. He thought she would do better at home with him and Brendan. Brendan would be the best medicine for her; the wee fellow would lift her spirits.

How was she? he asked. Not bad. They sat for a bit holding hands, saying nothing, avoiding one another's eyes.

"Sadie," he began, thinking how difficult it was even to begin.

"Yes?"

"I've been thinking . . ." Haltingly, he told her what he had thought on his walk.

"I've been thinking too," she said, and told him what she had thought in the night.

"It's difficult."

She nodded.

"But we must try . . . to understand the differences."

"I don't think I'd ever want to be a Catholic but I'll try not to hate you being one. Or Brendan either.

"Thank you." He squeezed her hand. "It's harder for you than me, I'm thinking."

Her church didn't mean as much to her as his did to him, she recognised; since leaving Belfast she seldom thought to go. She never had enjoyed going much, had done it under protest at the insistence of her mother who would never miss a Sunday, and whenever possible had mitched and roamed the street of Belfast, or idled around the docks looking at the big ships wishing she was on them. Her religion might not mean too much but she knew that deep down the attitudes instilled by her mother and father were still pretty strong. She had, after all, been brought up with King Billy on the gable end of their house!

"What are you smiling about?"

"Just thinking of the old days . . . the street and that. It was good fun then. But I could never go back."

"We've come a long way, the both of us!"

And they both knew there was a fair way to go yet. Talking was easier than doing.

After Kevin's visit Sadie felt easier. She still had a pain in her heart over the loss of her baby but she felt that something essential had happened between her and Kevin. She felt as if she had crossed a line, a frontier, and when she looked back over it to Christmas Eve she saw herself as someone different. In that short time she had changed, not drastically of course (she smiled at that idea), but importantly.

On New Year's Eve she was allowed home. Snow covered the ground, the hills beyond, and the sun shone brightly making the whole world sparkle. Another new year was coming in, thought Sadie, as Kevin turned in at the Sullivans' gates, and where would they be at the end of it? They could not stay here indefinitely, live with the Sullivans even if Kevin went on working for them. They felt at home, but it was not their home.

They were met by Gerald and Clodagh, the Sullivans and of course Brendan. Sadie went for him straightaway, scarcely noticing the others, scooping him up into her arms and hugging him tight.

"Have you been a good boyo then?"

"No," he shouted, crowing with pleasure, patting the sides of her face with his hands.

He followed her around for the rest of the day, would not leave her side, even going with her to bed when she took a rest in the afternoon.

Whilst Sadie and Brendan were sleeping Kevin worked outside sawing up logs. Clodagh passed him on her way down the drive, saying that he was never done working, did he never feel like taking a rest? He supposed not. He liked to be on the move, was not one to sit hugging the fire or lying on the settee reading racing magazines. Like Gerald. Gerald would be leaving in a day or two, to return to his stable in Ireland. And Clodagh? When would she be leaving? Kevin had told Mr Sullivan that he hoped to find other accommodation for her in the village shortly but he had no idea where for nearly everyone knew Clodagh and few would fancy her as a lodger.

She had another boyfriend now, called Jack Williams. Kevin knew him from the pub. He was different from Cliff: older for a start, about ten years senior to Clodagh, rather slow in his speech and movements, and there was nothing of the tearaway about him. He worked at a farm further down the valley and was known to a good, reliable worker. He did not seem the type to appeal to Clodagh. When Kevin passed some comment to this effect to her she shrugged and said he made a change, and, anyway, there wasn't much choice in a place like this.

Kevin straightened his back, stood for a few minutes looking out across the parkland smooth and white under its cloak of snow to the hills, facing in the direction of his little ruined cottage. For that was how he thought of it. His cottage. When he went to sleep at night he dreamt of it and them inside, and no man in black ever came to cry, "Out!"

He finished sawing, stacked the logs and tidied the yard as the sun was flooding the white hills with wild pinks and oranges. Such a sight made him feel it was good to be alive. He needed such sights in his life.

Sadie was reading a story to Brendan by the fire, Gerald was lying on the settee. They looked peaceful.

"I'll put the kettle on," said Kevin, putting his head round the door, "and we'll have a cup of tea."

"Bring some shortbread and Christmas cake," called Sadie.

It was changed days too to see Kevin going off to make the tea. When they had first married he had not wanted to do anything domestic, had not thought that he should, but since Brendan had been born he had changed his mind. He had been brought up not to help with 'woman's work', as his mother would have called it.

Sadie felt drowsy beside the warm fire. She heard her voice getting slower and slower and every now and then she had to stop to yawn. Brendan himself was almost asleep, his cheeks flushed, eyelids half closed, thumb in mouth. She stopped reading and he did not seem to notice.

The way you're brought up certainly stays with you for a very long time, she thought, as she gazed into the purple and orange flames licking the logs. Loyal Orange Lodge flames! The smell of the logs soothed her. She yawned again.

Clodagh came in, taking off her duffel coat and throwing it over the back of a chair. Her cheeks were bright pink from the cold, and her eyes were clear. She was a good-looking girl, thought Sadie, when she was not scowling.

"Kevin's making us a cup of tea."

"Good." Clodagh sat down cross-legged in front of the fire to warm her hands. "There's a taxi coming up the drive," she said casually.

"Must be visitors for the Sullivans," murmured Sadie.

When the sitting room door opened she only half looked up, thinking it was Kevin. But it was not Kevin: it was Mrs Sullivan.

"There's a visitor here for you, Sadie."

A visitor? Sadie struggled to her feet, easing Brendan off her leg where his head had been leaning. Kitty? Mrs Hignett? Maria? Quickly now she was coming awake. She hurried after Mrs Sullivan into the hall.

There, standing beside the ressurected Christmas tree, stood her mother, wearing the same purple coat and hat that she had on her visit to them last year in Liverpool.

"Ma!" gasped Sadie.

Mrs Jackson nodded the purple hat. She was clutching her handbag to her chest, and beside her stood a suitcase.

"Yes, it's me, Sadie."

"How did you get here?"

"Oh I've had the most desperate time, I can tell you! I crossed over on the boat last night so I did and it's taken me the entire day to get here from Liverpool. I've been on trains, taxis, buses. And half of them the wrong ones. Nobody had ever heard of this place, let alone being able to pronounce it. I'd no idea you'd be living right at the back of beyond!"

Chapter Fourteen

"WELL then, and how are you?" demanded Mrs Jackson.

"Fine. At least—"

"You couldn't be fine after that ordeal you've been through." The purple hat trembled. "Dear, but it's a terrible thing to lose a child. Terrible!"

"Ma," began Sadie. She did not feel strong enough to cope with such a visit at such a time. If only her mother had let her get her strength back first!

"I'm here to look after you, Sadie, so you can relax now. Your da said to me, 'Away on over, Aggie, and look after the girl'. He paid my fare and all. See how much he thinks of you!"

In spite of her weakness and the feeling of shock at her mother's arrival, Sadie did feel impressed that her father was concerned for her. Since her marriage he had given no sign that he ever spared her a kind word. As an Orangeman he had been outraged, and had felt betrayed.

"Come on through then, Ma."

Sadie bent to lift the suitcase but her mother would not allow her to touch it, telling her that she must be careful, and give herself a decent chance to recover. It was as well she had come! No one else would have taken good enough care of Sadie, that was obvious. Before leaving the hall, Mrs Jackson glanced about her and up the red-carpeted staircase, commenting that this wasn't a bad place, once you got here.

"Pretty posh. Awful nice bit of carpeting that." She sniffed. Pity Linda Mullet couldn't have visited you in this!"

Sadie led her to the sitting room, glad to get her out of earshot of Mrs Sullivan. Not that she was too keen to get her into the earshot of Clodagh and Gerald, not to mention Kevin!

She opened the sitting room door. Kevin had not returned yet with the tea.

"Ma, this here's Clodagh, Kevin's sister. And this is Gerald, Kevin's brother. This is my mother."

Mrs Jackson eyed them and sniffed again, then said in a freezing voice that she was pleased to meet them. She kept her gloved hands clasped firmly in front of her, not that either Clodagh or Gerald would have expected to shake one of them.

Clodagh looked round and said, "Hi!" as if Mrs Jackson had been expected or lived round the corner. Gerald appeared a bit more interested, putting down his magazine and sitting up to take a better look.

Sadie diverted her mother's attention to Brendan, saying hadn't he grown and so forth? Mrs Jackson said she would have expected him to have grown, there would have been something funny if he had not in fifteen months. She added though that he was a fine looking boy, well built and sturdy.

"Come to Granny then." She held out her arms.

Brendan backed away.

"He's just wakened, Ma. He'll go to you later."

Eyeing the new arrival warily, Brendan ran for his mother.

"Look's like he's a real mother's boy."

"He's missed me being away in hospital."

The door opened to admit Kevin. He almost dropped the tray when he saw his mother-in-law standing there warming her back at the fire. A slight suggestion of steam was beginning to rise from the purple coat.

"Hello, Kevin."

"Oh—er, hello, Mrs Jackson." He could do nothing but stare.

"I had to come and see that Sadie was all right," said Mrs

Jackson in a voice that suggested that if she were not it could only be his fault. "And how are you yourself then, Kevin?"

"All right." He set down the tray.

"Could just be doing with a cup of tea," said Mrs Jackson, taking off her hat and her gloves. A bad sign, thought Sadie, for usually her mother kept her hat on until she decided if she would stay. Of course she had had such a long journey getting here and it would be such a long journey back to the boat that she would have no option. So they were to have yet another guest for New Year!

Mrs Jackson sat herself down by the fire, drank three cups of tea and ate two slices of cake and two pieces of shortbread, then she dusted the crumbs from her skirt and said that Sadie was not a bad wee baker. Not now.

"She must have learned more from me than I thought."

Neither Sadie nor Kevin said very much for the first hour after Mrs Jackson's arrival. They kept looking at one another, unbelievingly. It didn't seem possible, but it was true, she was here, in the flesh, in her best going-to-church clothes and her hair all set in ridges which had miraculously survived the journey. Dear but it had been a terrible crossing, they heard yet again, and she hadn't slept a wink the whole night through, had been tossed almost out of her bunk. She talked non-stop about the trials of getting here, the trials of living in Belfast, and the trials of having neighbours such as she had. She meant in particular Mrs Mullet, whose Linda had come back with plenty of fine tales.

"The things she said! I got a right red face so I did."

Sadie found her tongue then. She informed her mother that they weren't always able to choose how they lived, they'd had real bad luck with Mr Ellersley dying and getting put out of their cottage, and she didn't give a damn what Linda Mullet thought.

"O.K., keep your hair on! Sure I know you must be on edge at the moment, Sadie. It's only understandable!" Mrs Jackson sighed. "What desperate bad luck you've had, one way and another."

Kevin decided that he had better go and fetch more wood for the fire. Clodagh and Gerald also drifted out, leaving Sadie alone with her mother and her child. Brendan was restless and not at all taken by his grandmother in her purple coat sitting by the fire.

"You could have written and let us know you were coming," said Sadie.

Mrs Jackson had decided there was not much point in writing, and so had set out immediately. "For all I knew you might have been at death's door. After all, you are my daughter."

Sadie softened. "I know, Ma, and I'm right glad you've come. Honestly."

Mrs Jackson removed her coat and Sadie hung it in the wardrobe. She explained to her mother that they were rather tight for space, what with having Clodagh and Gerald here.

"What are you doing with those two living on your back? I think you've enough without another couple of McCoys to feed. The nerve of them!"

Sadie explained that Gerald was only here for a few days and they were hoping to find Clodagh somewhere else to live quite soon. She said that Mrs McCoy had plenty of trouble on her hands and Kevin felt it was the least he could do to help out with Clodagh.

Mrs Jackson sniffed. This habit of her mother never failed to make Sadie wince. For a moment she almost said something, then stopped herself.

"If them Catholics wouldn't have as many kids they wouldn't have as much trouble."

"Now, Ma, don't start. I know what you think about all that so you don't have to tell me again."

"I don't much fancy the look of either of them. You'd know at a glance they were Micks all right."

"Ma!" exploded Sadie.

"And them Sullivans that own the house? I saw they had a crucifix in the hall when I came in."

Sadie turned away. Her mother would notice that; she had an eye for such things.

"What a terrible thing, Sadie Jackson, you living in a house full of Catholics! Catholics the lot of them! And you brought up a good Protestant."

Sadie said that she had something cooking in the kitchen and left the room. Kevin was there, sitting by the stove, reading a newspaper. Sadie let off a tirade about her mother.

"Never mind, Sadie love, we'll just have to make the best of it."

Sadie said she was fed up making the best of things, of Clodagh, and never having their own house, and now her mother. And where were they all to sleep? There was nothing for it but to have her mother sleep with her in their bedroom and for Kevin to sleep in Brendan's room. Sadie groaned at the idea of sharing a bed with her mother.

Kevin was thinking of his own mother and that it was time he saw her again. Mrs Jackson had come twice to visit them but he could not expect his mother to make the journey, nor did he think it would be wise if she did. She and Sadie would never last a day under the same roof. He would have to go to Ireland to see her, he knew that. He must. And he hoped that Sadie would see that too. Mr Sullivan had said that he could spare him for a few days in February.

Sadie cooked a good meal for their New Year's Eve dinner, which even Mrs Jackson enjoyed and praised, and they opened a couple of bottles of cheap wine Kevin had bought in Chester. Mrs Jackson addressed herself almost entirely to Sadie, occasionally to Kevin, but never a word did she have for either Gerald or Clodagh.

Clodagh went off after dinner.

"A bit young to be going off like that, isn't she?" said Mrs Jackson.

She got no reply. Kevin began to wash the dishes and Sadie and Gerald to dry.

At midnight, they drank a toast to the New Year, and then Sadie went to bed with her mother. Mrs Jackson put her teeth in a glass of water beside the bed, saying that she had best keep them close beside her in case anything should happen to them. On her previous visit Kevin had tossed them into the sink and cracked them. Sadie prayed that nothing would happen to them here, they were too far from civilisation to get them mended easily, and her mother without teeth was ten times worse than with. She moaned and groaned as if she was at a wake.

Sadie slept scarcely at all. Mrs Jackson, presumably exhausted by her journey, slept heavily and snored constantly. The sound filled Sadie's head, making it throb, until she had to get up and go into the kitchen to take a drink of water. It was four o'clock in the morning and the house was dead silent.

Footsteps scraped on the path outside. Sadie looked at the door, watched it open and Clodagh came in.

"For heaven's sake, Clodagh—"

"Oh, don't start. It's New Year after all."

Clodagh shook the snow from her head and shoulders. She looked as if she had been drinking quite a lot, there was a glazed look about her eyes. She went past Sadie, out of the kitchen and into the sitting room.

Sadie returned to her mother whose snores could be heard right along the other end of the passage.

"How long are *you* staying for then?" Mrs Jackson asked Gerald over breakfast the next morning.

"I'll need to be off in a day or so."

"Aren't you going to go up to Liverpool while you're here, Gerald?" asked Sadie. "I thought you'd be going to see Maria?"

"Maria?" said Mrs Jackson. "Wasn't that that black girl that lived in your house in Liverpool?"

Sadie said yes, that Maria was West Indian. She looked at Gerald. He shrugged, went on eating his cornflakes, crunching them noisily, which made Mrs Jackson eye him with disapproval.

"Well?" demanded Sadie.

"I don't think I'm going to bother going to Liverpool." Gerald got up and walked out.

Honestly, thought Sadie, these McCoys! They were terrible at telling you what they were thinking, even Kevin. She herself was never able to keep anything to herself for more than a few minutes, but when Kevin had something on his mind he brooded. He had something on his mind now but would not say what. Well, why shouldn't he have a lot on his mind? he had said, when she had asked him.

Mrs Jackson sighed. "Aye, but you haven't an easy life, Sadie, that's for certain sure. I'm right sorry for you, that I am."

"You don't have to be." Sadie spoke tartly. She hated to receive pity, and her mother was the last one she wanted it from.

The snow was so thick that they could not even go out for a walk. It was possible to plough across the field in gumboots, but Mrs Jackson did not have gumboots with her and they had none to fit her, nor could she be imagined in a pair. She sat either in the kitchen or sitting room, wherever Sadie happened to be, and gave her a running commentary on life back in Belfast. Sadie did not mind that, quite enjoyed hearing the news; at least it was better than listening to her mother gripe about Kevin and his family.

Two day's later Gerald packed his holdall and was ready to go. He said he'd write and let them know how he was going on, then he gave Sadie a quick kiss on the cheek, nodded at her mother, and climbed into the van. Kevin was driving him to Ruthven on the first stage of his journey back to County Cork.

When Kevin came back Sadie said it had been all right having Gerald, she didn't mind him at all. "And I suppose it's nice for you to see your family too from time to time," she said with a grin.

Kevin hesitated.

"What is it then?" They were alone in their bedroom, for once.

"Sadie, I've been thinking—I think I'll have to go home and see my mother and the others sometime soon."

Sadie sighed. She hated the thought of him going back to Ulster, in the state that it was in, and to his mother, but she realised that he would have to go.

"I won't go yet, love. Not till you're stronger."

Kevin told Sadie that Gerald had talked to him about Maria. Gerald had decided that it would be better not to go and visit her, he had thought there was no point.

"How do you mean no point?" said Sadie. "I'm sure Maria will be terribly disappointed when she knows he was here."

"Gerald said there could be no future for them so he thought it was better to let it drop now."

Why shouldn't they have a future if they wanted one? said Sadie. Gerald was young, said Kevin, and he wasn't thinking of getting married and settled down yet. But Sadie was sorry for Maria. Kevin said Sadie was just a romantic at heart, but not everybody was as daft as they had been.

Gerald had also said to Kevin that when he saw what a struggle it was for him to keep a wife and child he had decided that it would be better to wait a while himself. He had plenty of time and was only an apprentice at the stable. Kevin did not pass on that bit of information to Sadie for that would have enraged her, and she would have seen it as some kind of slight to herself.

Kevin put his arms around Sadie. "I'm glad we were daft though—" He broke off as the door opened and his mother-in-law entered.

She stopped in the doorway. "I hope I'm not interrupting any-thing—"

"Of course not, Ma. Come on in, the more the merrier!"

"I could be doing with a cup of tea, Sadie. My throat's like the inside of a chicken coop."

Sadie went to the kitchen to put on the kettle followed by her mother who was quite capable of filling kettles herself. It was funny but her mother was acting almost as if she was one of her daughter's children, making demands and getting ratty if Sadie ignored her for more than a few minutes.

"I really don't know how you stick it here," said Mrs Jackson, gazing out over the snowy park. "It's like being on the moon. And you've hardly any friends of your own age, have you?"

"I've got Angelica and Matthew."

Mrs Jackson gave one of her sniffs. She had met them and been suspicious of their soft words and gentle smiles. They had told her that the only way that the problems of Ireland would be resolved was by love. Catholics and Protestants would have to learn to love one another.

"I know it's difficult, Mrs Jackson, even to think about," Ange-lica had said earnestly.

Difficult? Mrs Jackson's eyes had bulged. She had not been able to speak.

"But not impossible," Matthew had added.

"Here's your tea, Ma." Sadie set it on the table.

"You make the funniest friends, Sadie, really you do. I don't know where you pick them up. There were all them blacks in Liverpool—"

"Don't you ever give over? You go on like a leaking tap."

"Don't you dare speak to me like that, Sadie Jackson!"

"McCoy!"

And so a row started. Inevitably, they had a few during Mrs Jackson's visit; they were usually sharp and close to the bone, but did not last, mostly because Sadie could not hold a grudge for long. Usually she walked out of the room and by the time she came back had forgotten they had been quarrelling.

Mrs Jackson stayed ten days. Before she left she gave Sadie fifty one-pound notes secured with an elastic band.

"But, Ma, what's all this?" Sadie's eyes goggled.

"A wee nest egg for you. A woman needs a bit put by, just in case." Mrs Jackson spoke darkly, nodded knowingly, suggesting all manner of disasters.

"But where did you get it from?"

"You don't think I don't manage to put a bit by from my house-keeping every week, do you?"

Sadie's mother had always had a battery of jars and tins all over the house in which she tucked away pound notes and coins.

"Now don't you let on you've got it!"

Sadie, feeling dazed, thanked her mother, and put the notes in her dressing table drawer.

"You're looking better, Sadie. It's as well I came. I think I've put you back on the right road now."

They kissed, and Brendan suffered his grandmother to put her lips against his cheek. He had never quite come round to her.

"Look after yourself," called Mrs Jackson from the van.

"You too!"

Kevin was driving Mrs Jackson to Chester where she would catch the train to Liverpool.

When they had gone and Sadie put Brendan down for his nap, the house felt quiet and she felt lonely. Since she had come home she had hardly been on her own for a minute, and now that she was, all she could think of was the baby. She opened the drawer where she had put his clothes between tissue paper. If only—

Stop it, Sadie Jackson, no good will come of this!

She went to the kitchen, baked a cake and was taking it out of the oven when Kevin returned.

"The last ten days have felt like ten years," he said.

Sadie shrugged. "Ach, it wasn't too bad." She laid the cake on the draining board. "Guess what she gave us? Fifty pounds."

"Fifty pounds!" Kevin whistled. "That'll come in useful towards our house. It was right good of her to give it to us, so it was. I wish I'd known to thank her."

"I know she's a pain at times but—"

"She is your mother," finished Kevin, and smiled.

And into both of their minds came the thought of Kevin's mother.

Chapter Fifteen

KEVIN crossed to Ireland at the beginning of February. He had not been home for more than two years and as the boat sailed up Belfast Lough he could not but be a bit excited. Rain was sweeping the shore, blurring it, but he felt that he knew exactly what it was like. It was his, after all, his homeland.

In the bus, all the way to Tyrone, he could not take his eyes from the window. How green the countryside was. And how peaceful it looked. Deceptively.

His mother was expecting him. When he came in through the door she clasped him in her arms and would not leave go of him. She kept saying that she had never thought to see him again, it was like a miracle.

"Don't be silly, Ma. You knew full well I'd be back."

"I never knew any such thing. I didn't know if that wife of yours would let you come to me."

"Now, Ma, don't start." Kevin spoke gently, he was not angry with her. He was shocked to see how much she had aged, her hair had turned white and her face was lined and marked. "Sadie has nothing against me coming to see you." It was not altogether the truth but there was no need to be honest with his mother on that point. He and Sadie had had a bit of a scene before he left, when she had said he might have waited a while longer before leaving her. He had said that he was only leaving her for a week. And this was the most suitable time as far as Mr Sullivan was concerned for Kevin to be away.

The cottage had been cleaned for his homecoming until it shone. And his mother had been baking, soda bread, potato bread, date and walnut loaf, scones of all kinds, and several cakes.

"It's like the return of the prodigal son," laughed Brede, when she came in to see Kevin.

She had changed also, aged, though not so drastically as his mother of course. She had become plumper, slightly matronly almost, even though she was but twenty years old. Her third child had been born just before Christmas.

"Are you happy then, Brede?" asked Kevin.

She nodded. She said that Robert was a good husband to her and she had three fine children. The only worry in her life, apart from the troubles which were everybody's worry, was their mother. She took Kevin for a walk across the field. Their mother often acted strangely these days, getting worked up about nothing at all and imagining things. She was not easy to deal with and Brede was troubled for the younger children. It was not all that good an up-bringing for them.

Kevin said that he had gathered as much, and had realised that his mother had turned a bit odd in the past few years. Ever since his father had died.

"Of course her life was never easy, even before that," said Brede. "With all of us to bring up and not much money."

"I wish I could help more. But the truth is, Brede, I can't. I have Sadie and Brendan. And Clodagh now—"

"I'm sure Clodagh's doing rightly with you though," said Brede quickly, clearly not wishing to have him say that he wanted to send Clodagh back. Brede and Clodagh had never got on too well: they were opposites. Kevin saw that it would not be possible to send Clodagh back, that she would not stay anyway. But he had to make sure that none of the others were sent after her, which was what Sadie feared. She had said he must tell his mother that she should not send anyone else. He must tell his mother plainly and get her to acknowledge that she understood.

Even as he was walking with Brede, his mother was calling after him, willing him to return to her side.

"I've hardly seen you this past few years, I'm not wanting to waste a minute of you now you're back."

"I can only stay a week, Ma."

"Ah, sure you can stay a little bit longer than that, son. God only knows when I'll see you again. If I ever do."

"Of course you will."

Kevin told her that he had a job to keep, she must understand that. She did not appear to understand, would not listen, kept saying that he should write and ask Mr Sullivan to let him stay a while longer. "Tell him your mother's ill and needs you. It's nothing but the God's own truth."

Michael, the next brother in line to Gerald, was working on the farm and doing well. He was a fine steady boy and Kevin had no worries over him. He had always been that way, apart from a spell when he had been under Gerald's influence and run wild a little, but that stage was behind him. When Kevin spoke to him about their mother Michael said that she was a bit of a bother at times, but she was getting old. He did not seem to realise how sick his mother actually was, in her mind. Perhaps it was just as well, thought Kevin, he would manage better that way.

The rest of the children were still at school and as far as Kevin could tell were doing all right. Kathleen, the next girl after Clodagh, was more like Brede, he fancied. She was quiet, sat reading or sewing in the kitchen, and seemed to have none of Clodagh's restlessness.

Whilst Kevin was at home there was a shooting incident nearby, in which someone died, and in the town a bomb went off in a pub killing two, injuring seven. Kevin found himself tensing every time he went into a village or town or sat in a pub with Robert, his brother-in-law. He was no longer used to this, had forgotten what it was like to be for ever looking over your shoulder or under your feet.

"You can't afford not to keep your eyes peeled," said Robert.

It was their way of life.

When would it ever end? No one could begin to answer that. It was one of those questions that lay in the back of everyone's mind but wasn't worth voicing. Kevin wished that he could take them all and bring them back with him to the estate in Wales, far away from all this trouble and violence. But he knew that even if he could they would not want to come. And he grinned when he thought of Sadie's face if he was to drive up to the back door with the van full of McCoys.

He wrote her one letter telling her that everyone was more or less all right, except for his mother. He said that Ireland was looking fine and bonny even in the month of February with the wind howling and the rain pouring. He said it was nice to be back.

"Do you think you'll ever come home for good?" asked Brede hopefully.

Kevin shrugged. That was another of the questions that seemed to have no answer. He could not say.

"I suppose you can't," said Brede, whose life was predictable, more or less. She would probably stay on the farm till the end of her days. Robert had a good job, his father was farm manager and there would be little reason for them to move. Robert had no ambitions to set sail for Canada or Australia or anything like that and Brede was content to have it that way.

On the day before he was due to leave Kevin sat in the kitchen with his mother drinking tea. Sleet was falling outside drowning the fields and trees and the farmhouse beyond. It was cosy in the kitchen with a good fire going in the range and the smell of warm baking coming from the oven. Kevin had sat and watched his mother make a batch of soda bread and potato bread. It had been like old times, sitting in the kitchen watching her hands move deftly, slapping the dough, tipping out the flour. When he watched her like this she seemed to become the mother of his childhood again. Even her face looked different, softer, more relaxed, less worried. It gave him a knot in his throat to see her like this and he wished that he could make her be like this for the rest of her life. He sighed.

"Whatever are you sighing for, son? Sure you're too young to be so weighted down."

Young? Did she think that really? He spoke to her gently,

teasingly. He was a married man now, with a child. Now it was her turn to sigh. Before she could speak, Kevin got in first.

"Ma, you know I've got to be on my way tomorrow? I must. So don't ask me to stay. Please!"

The soft look was gone from her face now, and back had come the irritated, cantankerous frown.

"I would stay if I could, Ma. But it isn't possible." He got up and stood looking out of the window, with his back to the kitchen. He knew for certain that he did not want to come back and live here in the midst of his family. If he came back to Ireland it would not be to this place: he would find his own.

"Kevin."

He looked round. She was taking something from a drawer. She came to him.

"Here, son, I want you to have this." She pressed the object into his hand.

He felt the shape of the piece of wood, knowing at once what it was without having to look. His fingers clenched it close against the palm of his hand.

"Thanks, Ma."

"It was your father's."

He nodded. He put the wooden cross into his pocket.

There was a car coming up the drive, an invalid car. It turned in at the front of the cottages.

"Who's this, Ma?"

"For dear sake, it's your Uncle Albert!"

"Uncle Albert!" Kevin dived to the door, tugging it open and letting a gust of cold wet wind swirl into the warm kitchen.

The car had come to rest outside the front door, and sure enough there was Uncle Albert sitting behind the wheel.

"Uncle Albert," Kevin repeated again, shaking his head. Uncle Albert had been injured in the same pub bombing that had killed his father and had had his legs blown off. He had imagined Uncle Albert confined to bed or a chair in the house. But here he was sitting at the wheel of a car. Uncle Albert had always loved cars, ancient ones, that had been tied up with string and always stopped at the most awkward moments. His cars had been notorious in the district.

Kevin dashed up the path and opened the driver's door.

"Well, lad, it's great seeing you! I heard you were here so thought I'd take a turn down."

It was great to see him too, Kevin assured him, really great. He helped him out of the car and down the path. Uncle Albert had two sticks and managed well in spite of the skiddy wet path.

"That's a fine smell of baking you have there, Mary. And you've a cup of tea on the boil, I see."

"Well, and how are you then, Uncle Albert?" Kevin demanded.

"Not so bad. Considering." They were quiet for a moment, all thinking of Kevin's father. It was better to be alive without legs, Kevin presumed, than not to be alive at all, though at the time it had happened he had thought himself that Uncle Albert would have been better off dead. Mrs McCoy forgot her own troubles, bustled about the kitchen making fresh tea and buttering hot soda bread straight from the oven. She asked about Uncle Albert's wife and their children and neighbours. They still lived in their old district of Belfast. And Uncle Albert wanted to know all about Kevin and Sadie and his child and their life.

"Aye, you're well out of it, son. If I could get out I'd do the same. But how can I?"

"Sure what would you do in England, Albert?" asked Mrs McCoy. "You've lived in the same street all your life, so you have."

Uncle Albert chuckled. "You're right there, Mary. Maybe it wouldn't be as easy to take to a fresh place at my time of life. And with these two lumps of wood at the end of me." He tapped his legs. "They're a great pair of legs, Kevin boy. They get me around right enough."

"Up and down to the pub no doubt," said Mrs McCoy. "I bet you manage that rightly."

"'Deed I do. Life wouldn't be worth living otherwise, would it now?"

Mrs McCoy shook her head. Legs or no legs, Albert would never change. Kevin asked him if he wasn't afraid to go back into pubs, in case of another bomb.

"Ach, you can't sit at home doing nothing all day. You just have to take a chance on it. You could end up afraid of your own shadow, so you could. I reckon I haven't got much left to lose now, eh?" Uncle Albert laughed again, but Kevin could not join in.

Mrs McCoy served lunch and afterwards Brede came in with her children and the afternoon developed into a party. Kevin, in the midst of them, found himself happy and at ease with his family for the first time in several years. He was glad that he had come; it was necessary to do so from time to time, to renew the bonds.

When night was approaching Uncle Albert declared that he'd best be on his way. He'd promised his wife that he'd be home before dark.

"But she knows me, of course."

Would he be all right on his own in the dark in this bad weather? asked Kevin. But Uncle Albert was always all right as long as he was in a car. Kevin and Brede took him down the path to the car. The rest of the children gathered in the lighted doorway to wave him off.

"Well, Kevin lad, see you again sometime no doubt."

"Certainly I hope so. You know you're welcome to come over and take a holiday with us any time you like?"

"I might take you up on that and all. I just might. I could be doing with a wee bit of a holiday."

Uncle Albert put the key in the starter, turned it. Nothing happened. This had been routine when he had his old cars, the ones tied up with string, but this was fairly new. It had been given to him after his accident.

"Drat the thing!"

Uncle Albert tried again and again. A child giggled from the doorway and was hissed at by Mrs McCoy. Kevin too wanted to laugh. Wait till he told Sadie about this!

"Will I give you a push then, Uncle Albert?"

"I think you'll have to."

Unfortunately they were not on a slope as they used to be in their old street. As Uncle Albert said, that had been dead useful at times. The path, too, in front of the cottages was muddy with the sleet which had fallen all day and was still drifting down soaking their heads. Robert came to help Kevin and together they managed to turn the car round and push it to the end of the drive. There was still no sign of life inside the engine.

Uncle Albert shook his head. "It must be the sleet. It's a devil that. That's what's doing it right enough."

They began to push, moving the car steadily along the road outside the farm. It was completely flat also so there was little joy to be had in trying to get any speed up. But the car was light and Kevin and Robert were strong so they were able to shove it along at a fair rate. They had to run.

"We'll soon be in Belfast if we go on at this rate," said Robert, puffing. The sleet was thickening, turning to snow. When they had gone about half a mile, Robert and Kevin stopped. Their eyebrows and lashes were fringed with white.

Uncle Albert was scratching his head under his cap. "I can't think what can be wrong with this damned machine. Sure it's never done this on me before."

Kevin gazed through the eddying snow. "There don't seem to be any of your handy friends around, Uncle Albert." In the old days there had always been friends of Uncle Albert who appeared at the right moment, ready to help or tow.

What was to be done? They couldn't push the car all the way to Belfast. There was nothing else for it, said Robert, but to take Uncle Albert back to the house. They would be soaked if they stood there much longer.

Puffing and panting now, and facing into the driving snow, they propelled the car back along the road, through the gateway into the drive and back to the cottage. The door opened, out spilled the younger children.

Mrs McCoy declared that Albert would just have to stay the night. They could manage for beds, one way or another; they always had. And Robert suggested that they send a telegram to his wife to let her know he was all right, otherwise she might be worried sick. There were too many reasons in this province for a man not to come back at night.

Robert phoned the message from the farmhouse; Uncle Albert took off his coat and settled in for the evening. And it was a great evening they had too, to match the afternoon.

"There's always a silver lining, isn't that right?" said Uncle Albert, seated by the fire with a pint of Guiness in his hand.

Kevin sat up late with him after the others had gone to bed. They talked about all sorts of things, about Kevin's father and the old days, and about Sadie too. Uncle Albert had met Sadie and liked her. He thought she was a grand wee girl, full of fire and spirit.

"Sure I was never against your marriage, Kevin. If you're happy that's the main thing. It's rare these days, I'm thinking. It's lucky you are, lad. And don't be forgetting that!"

They slept for a few hours, sharing the kitchen. And in the morning they got up to eat ham and eggs with a stack of potato bread fried by Mrs McCoy. Kevin must leave shortly on his journey back to Wales, and Uncle Albert must try to get on the road to Belfast.

Robert arrived, shaking his head and grinning. "I found out what was wrong with your car, Uncle Albert."

"Have you indeed? You're a smart lad, Robert, that you are!"

"You'd no petrol in the tank."

Kevin burst out laughing. Sadie would certainly enjoy this latest tale of Uncle Albert when he recounted it to her.

Chapter Sixteen

SADIE looked through the falling snow at the two policemen standing on the back step. The news they had brought was quite believable.

"Do you think—" The policeman looked up at the sky.

"Come on in."

They scraped their boots on the mat and followed her into the kitchen.

"Cup of tea?"

They said they wouldn't mind, it would put a bit of warmth back into them. They brushed the snowflakes from their shoulders and seated themselves in front of the range. Sadie, busying herself with the business of making tea, thought about the news they had brought. Clodagh had been caught shoplifting. It would have to happen when Kevin was away!

She poured the tea and sat down herself. They gave her the details, telling her how Clodagh had been caught lifting several articles from a store. They reeled off the list, making Sadie's head reel. A handbag, two silk scarves, a cashmere sweater, make-up, perfume, and a few other odds and ends.

"For dear sake!" cried Sadie. Her mind gagged at the idea of anyone taking all that lot. "Where had she put it?"

In a shopping bag. As bold as brass she had been, stuffing the things in and getting ready to walk out. And then she had been stopped by the store detective who had followed her around. He had noticed her in the shop before, had suspected that she had taken things but hadn't managed to catch her. Sadie shook her head and drank her tea. She had put in an extra spoonful of sugar, feeling she had need of it.

"You'd no idea at all, did you?"

Sadie shook her head, feeling a little guilty, for it was not strictly true; she had sometimes suspected for Clodagh often seemed to have new things. But what could she, Sadie, have done? Clodagh denied everything.

"I'm afraid we'll have to search the house."

"But you can't! I mean not the whole house—"

"Just your quarters then, Mrs McCoy. I understand that the rest of the place belongs to Mr Sullivan. I don't think we need trouble him."

Thank goodness for that at least! Sadie eyed the two policemen whom she noticed were eyeing her. Did they suspect that she was an accomplice? Or a receiver of stolen goods? She supposed they were entitled to think what they wanted to. After all, didn't Clodagh live with them? Drat you, Kevin McCoy, she said to herself, for being away and having a family such as yours!

The men got up. They thanked her for the cup of tea and set the empty cups on the table.

"Where would you like to start?"

They thought they might as well start here. Sadie said that they would find nothing in the kitchen. After all, it was Mrs Sullivan's kitchen even though she herself did not spend much time in it. Ah well, they said, you never know. When people were in this game they got up to all sorts of tricks.

Sadie stood beside the range, her arms folded, scowling at the two dark blue backs. They had come with their search warrant, she couldn't stop them searching but hated to see them raking in their belongings. She knew that they were just doing their job and probably didn't like it much either. They were wasting their time, she wanted to tell them, but forced herself to stay quiet. She knew what Kevin would say if he was here. It was best to say as little as possible. But if she could have got her hands on Clodagh she'd have half killed her. The girl was being held at the police station but would be released on a small amount of bail.

One of the policemen, the shorter of the two, sat back on his haunches in front of a cupboard. "Well now," he said slowly, "what have we here?" And out of the cupboard he lifted an old cardboard shoe box. He took off the lid and there inside was masses and masses of jewellery. Cheap stuff, not diamonds or anything like that, but no doubt worth some money, and undoubtedly stolen.

"Oh no!" cried Sadie.

They proceeded to the other rooms, the sitting room, Sadie and Kevin's bedroom, and Brendan's room. There was nothing in Sadie and Kevin's room but in the other two they found several things. Clothes, shoes, a couple of watches, a cigarette lighter. Sadie's throat went so dry she could hardly speak.

"I suppose you didn't know anything about any of this, Mrs McCoy?"

"Nothing. Honest."

"We'll need to ask you a few more questions of course. It's a pity your husband isn't here."

"It is indeed," she said.

"I take it he is coming back? From Ireland?"

"Coming back? Of course he is. Why wouldn't he?"

They shrugged. They took out their notebooks.

She told them when Clodagh had come to stay with them, gave her home address in Ireland and other details they asked for. At the police station Clodagh had said she was eighteen.

"She's only turned sixteen. Last week. She's a terrible liar that one," said Sadie. "I don't know why. Except that she's had a rotten life, you know, in Ireland with the bombing and all that."

Ah well, the policeman were sympathetic, but that didn't give you the right to break the law, to take property that wasn't yours. Sadie agreed.

"And so Mrs Mary McCoy is still the girl's legal guardian, is that right?"

That was right, Sadie confirmed, but they wouldn't get much

joy out of her. She wasn't in too much of a state to take charge of a girl like Clodagh.

"And are you? You don't look that old yourself."

Sadie felt ninety that snowy cold January afternoon, sitting beside the fire answering the policemen's questions. They said a social worker would come and talk to her, to get a picture of Clodagh's background. That would help the juvenile court to decide her fate.

Family background! Clodagh's scarcely bore thinking about.

She was kept in a remand home until the hearing would come up at the juvenile court. The social worker, when she came to visit Sadie, said that they had decided it would be best. Not only for Clodagh, but for Sadie too.

"You've a lot on your hands for a girl of your age. You were young marrying, weren't you?"

Sadie agreed that she was. But she had no regrets. None.

"That's nice then, dear."

"Though there are times . . ." began Sadie and stopped. Well, of course, there would be times that were difficult. At any age.

The social worker was easy to talk to and Sadie spent the whole afternoon spilling out the story of the Jacksons and the McCoys, of her courtship in Belfast with Kevin, and their exile in London, Liverpool, Cheshire and now here.

"Kevin and I had nothing to do with her stealing. You must believe that. We'd never take anything that wasn't ours."

"I believe you. Clodagh said herself that you knew nothing about it."

Sadie sat back on her seat. That was good at least, that Clodagh had not tried to pass any of her guilt on to them. No indeed, said the woman; she had been very anxious to say that her brother and his wife should not be involved.

"But you are involved, aren't you, Sadie? After all, she lives with you. The question is what are we to do with her?"

The social worker thought that it was too much for Sadie and Kevin to be responsible for Clodagh if she was to be released on probation. What was the alternative? asked Sadie. To stay in the remand home apparently. Sadie could not imagine Clodagh incarcerated in an institution.

"Perhaps not," said the social worker. "But she's done something wrong and she has to pay for it."

If she had a good home and someone to be responsible for her, she would probably be released on probation. Sadie told the social worker she had better come back and talk to Kevin when he came home. He would want a say in what was to happen to Clodagh. He was due the following day.

He came, and within half an hour had the full details. Sadie talked non-stop.

He went that same afternoon to see the social worker and told her that in no way could he be responsible for his sister Clodagh on probation. It would not be fair to his wife and he had to think of her first. He was fond of his sister right enough and if he were on his own—but he wasn't.

The social worker nodded.

Kevin went to see Clodagh. She shrugged, was cool, said little. Aren't you sorry? he asked her. Sorry she was caught, she said.

"You don't really mean that. You're not *that* hard, Clodagh." She shrugged again, and he said urgently, "Look at me, Clodagh. Don't you want to lead a decent life?"

She looked into his eyes, and he saw in hers a lost, almost frightened look, one that he had never seen before.

"You don't have to carry on this way, you know. You can change. You *must* change, Clodagh."

"Depends what you mean by decent life, doesn't it? I'm not wanting to slave my guts out like you."

"I'd rather do that and be able to face myself in the mirror."

"Well, I've had enough of it at home, all that scrimping and scraping. And Ma going on about all the mouths to feed."

"But *you* don't have all those mouths to feed. You've only got your own. You could work, you don't have to steal."

When he left her he did not know whether he had made any impression or not, whether he had got through. He knew inside himself that if anyone could, it would be him. Clodagh did listen to him, she seemed to care about his opinion and to feel something for him. She was fond of him, he knew it. He felt it. His heart was as heavy as a ball of lead as he drove back to the Sullivans' house.

He attended the hearing at the juvenile court, Sadie waited for him in a nearby café with Brendan. Evidence was given, Clodagh questioned, the social worker asked for her report. Clodagh was sullen and would not say more than the required minimum. Why had she taken the things? Because she had wanted them. Did she not know it was against the law? Of course. Why then? They did not get too far.

At the end of it all they said that it looked like they would have to send her to a remand home, they had no alternative. If she had had a good home they would have probably placed her on probation, since this was a first offence. Clodagh suddenly wakened up; she took a letter from her pocket.

"What if I was to get married?"

Well, *if* she got married—though she couldn't do that without her parent's consent before the age of eighteen—she could most likely be put on probation, providing the husband was a suitable person to look after her. Was she thinking of marrying?

"As a matter of fact I am. He's called Jack Williams, he's twenty-six years old, and he works on a farm near my brother." She took a sheet of paper from the envelope. "I wrote to my mother and she's given her consent." She passed the letter to the magistrate.

Kevin wanted to leap to his feet, seize the letter and tear it to shreds. His mother had no right to give permission, she knew nothing about this man, or what her daughter felt about him. All she wanted was to be rid of the responsibility of Clodagh. It was not right! But how could he say so? His mother was Clodagh's legal guardian, and was entitled to give consent.

"He's outside now," said Clodagh.

Jack was brought in and questioned. He confirmed that he wanted to marry Clodagh, he had a cottage, a steady job, a good wage, and he was prepared to be responsible for her. He made a good impression on the court: Kevin saw that. And marriage to such a man might steady her, that was bound to run in their minds, though he himself, knowing Clodagh, doubted it.

The court was adjourned for a few minutes and when they

reassembled the magistrate announced that Clodagh was to be placed on probation, providing that she did marry Jack Williams and reported regularly to the social worker.

Kevin left the court and went to Sadie.

"Clodagh's getting married? You're having me on!"

"I wish I were."

"Is she just doing it to get out of being sent to the remand home?"

"God knows! I can do nothing more about it, Sadie, nothing. We'll have to leave her to get on with her own life. Oh, we'll be near by if she needs us, but there isn't much else we can do."

"No," said Sadie slowly, "there isn't. Gerald was a different bag of beans entirely. But Clodagh—"

When they returned home Kevin went to the bedroom and took his father's crucifix from the drawer where he had buried it under a pile of clothes. He stood with it in his hand looking at the wall beside the bed, at his side. Could he put it there? What would Sadie say? But the crucifix had been his father's and was now his and should be hung up, not hidden away.

He fetched a nail and hammer.

"What are you doing?" asked Sadie, coming in, drawn by the sound of the banging.

He lifted the crucifix from his pocket and hung it on the nail. She looked. She did not say a word.

"It was my father's."

"I see."

"Do you mind?"

"I'm not sure."

"Can I leave it?"

After a moment she said, "Yes, I suppose so. If you want to."

"I do."

"I'll try—I'll try to get used to it."

Whenever she came into the room now it was the first thing she saw. It drew her eyes like a magnet. It seemed to tower, to grow bigger as she looked, to leer at her. It was only six inches high, four across, with a tiny replica of Christ crucified attached to it; yet it dominated the room.

She would have to ask Kevin to take it down: she hated the sight of it. She did not ask him.

It was only a piece of wood, she told herself, or two pieces, crossed. But it was a symbol: for her, a Catholic symbol. No decent Protestant reared in the North of Ireland would have a crucifix on his wall! Her ma would take a heart attack if she were to see it.

But her ma was not here to see it. And her ma was not married to Kevin. Her opinion did not have to be considered, or even called to mind. It was she, Sadie, who lived here and was married to Kevin.

She went close up to the crucifix and stood looking at it. Did it matter that much? Need it? She remembered Christmas Day and her promise to Kevin and to herself. There was nothing in a wooden cross that could harm her and if it made Kevin happy then that was sufficient reason for it to be there.

The next day, the crucifix was gone.

"Did you take it down?" she asked Kevin.

He nodded.

"Why?"

"I decided it wasn't fair to you. I was expecting too much."

"I don't mind. Really. You can put it back."

"No, I don't need to. I have it and that is enough."

They went to Clodagh's wedding; they were the only witnesses. They left Brendan and Tamsin with Angelica and Matthew. Jack said his family were all in South Wales, couldn't get away. Afterwards, they went for a drink in a hotel lounge where they sat for an hour not knowing where to look, not knowing what to talk about. Even Sadie. She asked Jack about his family, didn't learn much. He had little to say for himself but he seemed fond of Clodagh, they thought. And was she of him? She stared out of the window looking bored.

At the end of the hour she said, "Let's split, Jack!"

Kevin had intended to take them out for lunch but it no longer seemed a good idea. He did not mention it.

Clodagh and Jack were going to Blackpool for a week's

honeymoon. Sadie and Kevin watched them drive off.

"And the best of luck," said Sadie. "He'll need it."

Kevin took her hand. "Come on, I'm taking you out to lunch, love."

They had lunch at the hotel—Kevin said, "Never mind the expense for once!"—and remembered their own wedding day. They'd been in London, gone up to the West End for a meal and to the cinema, and eaten beans on toast for the rest of the week.

"Now then," said Kevin, "I'm taking you for a drive next. I've something to show you."

Chapter Seventeen

KEVIN drove the van carefully round the winding narrow road, narrowly clipping the hedge on the left hand side from time to time.

"I don't often come along here," said Sadie. "Doesn't go anywhere, does it?"

"Except Lewis's farm."

"It's pretty though."

"You like it?"

"Uhuh. The snowdrops are coming out, look, Kev!"

Kevin was stopping. He turned in through a gap in the hedge and brought the van to rest in front of the ruined cottage. Snowdrops were flowering all around it peppering the wild green grass with white.

"What are we stopping here for?"

He pointed.

"The old cottage?"

He nodded. "Let's get out."

Puzzled, she climbed down and followed him into the ruin. A rabbit scurried in front of them flashing its tail and then was gone legging it over the field.

"What do you think then, Sadie?"

"How do you mean?"

"This cottage? Would you fancy it?"

She gazed up through the hole in the roof, at the birds' nests, down the broken walls to the empty window holes to the weeds on the floor.

"Do you mean—living here like?"

"Oh, not as it is—"

"I'm relieved to hear that! Kevin, you're not serious? About us living here?"

"'Deed I am. Dead serious. I've had my eye on the place for months. And I've had a word with Mr Lewis. He'd be willing to let us have it and an acre of ground to go with it for a thousand pounds."

"A thousand pounds! But we haven't got that."

"We have three hundred though now. Sit down and I'll tell you my plan."

"Where?" She gazed about.

"The window sills make handy seats, so they do."

They sat down. Kevin put his arm round her and told her that he had made arrangements to get a mortgage from the district council which was keen to have old properties restored.

"We've enough for a deposit, you see. In fact, we wouldn't have to put down everything we've got, we could keep a bit for doing the place up."

"Doing the place up," echoed Sadie, who was still stunned. "It'd take more than we have to do it up. There isn't a wall standing. Hey, I wonder what me ma would say to this?" She grinned.

But they would get a grant to help do it up, Kevin explained, for things like wiring and plumbing, and installing a bathroom and kitchen. He intended to do all the work himself, felt quite capable of it, and that would bring the cost down a lot. He would do a bit at a time, as they could afford it.

"It'd take years."

"Oh, I don't know. We can go on living with the Sullivans anyway—I've talked to him about it—and I thought in the summer we could park the bus up here and live beside it."

"That might be nice," said Sadie, turning to look out at the hills. Slowly, it was dawning on her that it would be their very own place. "You're a deep one, Kevin McCoy, keeping this to yourself all this time and saying nothing!"

He had wanted to look into it all carefully, find out the ways and means before he put it to her.

"So what do you say then, Sadie?" He was solemn, unsmiling.

"Well, why not?" She was smiling. "It could be a real gas building our own house. I'll help you with the labouring. I'm sure I'd be a dab hand at the cement mixing!"

Kevin seized her by the shoulders and kissed her. "I don't know what I'd do without you."

"Your life would be a sight easier though, wouldn't it?"

He shook his head. She wrinkled her nose at him and made him smile. He could hardly speak now. The cottage had meant so much to him that he had had to wait until everything was more or less fixed before putting it to her. If she had scorned the idea it would have dejected him entirely. He had preferred to keep it as a dream, until he felt sure his plan could work. But he should have known that she would be with him. Wasn't she always? Even with Clodagh she had been willing to try.

"I ask an awful lot of you, Sadie."

She looked surprised. "But I do from you too, Kev. Isn't that the way of it?"

He nodded.

He told her how he imagined the lay-out of the house, and as he talked she saw the place roofed, floored, glazed, plastered. It took quite a bit of imagining as the wind whistled through the numerous openings making them huddle closer together for warmth, but imagine it she did, even with a log fire in the grate and curtains (woven by Angelica's friend?) at the windows.

"And I shall put straw mats on the floor." She felt a rush of excitement. "Oh Kevin, it'll be ours! And nobody'll be able to take it from us."

"Unless we don't pay the mortgage!"

But Kevin would see to it that they did, she knew that. And already her mind was ticking over with various schemes. She could breed from Tamsin, sell the puppies, keep hens, sell eggs, crochet shawls. . . .

"We're getting a real bargain, you know," said Kevin. "Mr Lewis could have got far more from someone wanting to make it into a holiday house. But he said he preferred to let people like us have it who need a home and would live in it all year round."

"What a lovely man!"

A squall of rain blew up suddenly, swept around the cottage and sent a flurry of water down upon them.

"We seem to have a bit of a leak," said Kevin, glancing upwards.

They ran for the van, where they sat watching the rain lash their cottage. When it rained up here it did it properly.

"I think the first thing will be to get the roof on," murmured Kevin.

It would be a lot of work getting the place in order, he knew that full well, a lot of muscle-pulling, back-breaking work, and there would be times when he would wish that he had never set eyes on the thing, times when they'd run out of money, times when they would wonder if they were mad. But if they persevered, and had even a little bit of luck, they could make it.

Just to own the land that it was on would be something! He smiled to himself as he gazed out over the wild overgrown piece of ground in which even to grow vegetables would be a challenge. But they could graze a beast perhaps, keep hens and ducks. It would be a start. And if ever they wanted to move from this district they would have it to sell and then money to take with them for the next beginning. They would have something to trade. They would not be such total hostages to fortune.

Glancing sideways, he watched Sadie gazing out at the rain and their new home. She looked serious. She was picking up gradually from the loss of the baby though still at times he caught her, off-guard, with a kind of bruised look in her eyes. He put his arm round her shoulders.

"Just like a wee palace, eh?"

She laughed. "I doubt if me ma would use the words about that! Linda Mullet's bungalow, yes. This, no!"

"Shall we go and fetch the wee fella then?"

They drove to Angelica and Matthew's where Tamsin lay

sleeping before the log fire and Brendan was playing on the kitchen floor with a large piece of clay. He was filthy, and disinclined to leave.

"No," he said, when Sadie held out his duffel coat. It was one word that he could say very clearly.

Sadie told Angelica and Matthew all about their cottage.

"How marvellous, Sadie!" said Angelica. "I'm so happy for you."

"If there's anything we can do to help?" said Matthew.

"Wait till you see it," said Sadie, "and then you might be wishing you'd never offered."

"Come on then, son." Kevin swung Brendan upwards ignoring his protests. "You're dead tired, aren't you?"

"He's been an absolute angel," declared Angelica.

"I'm glad to hear it," said Sadie, who normally had other words for him.

As they were turning in at the Sullivans' driveway on the way home they almost collided with a car coming in the opposite direction which also had designs on entering the drive.

"Jack!" gasped Sadie, who had been flung against Kevin. The ride had been so short that she had not bothered to fasten her safety belt.

Kevin was getting out, making for Jack. Sadie followed.

"Where's Clodagh?" Kevin peered into Jack's car.

"I dunno." Jack looked bewildered, as if he had been struck between the eyes.

"What do you mean?"

"She did a bunk. In Liverpool. Went to the *Ladies*, never came out."

"She might still be in there," said Sadie. "Lying on the floor, unconscious."

He shook his head. "I asked the attendant. After a bit. Well, I sat for ten minutes or so, couldn't understand it . . ." He scratched his head. "She said Clodagh had gone out the other way." He still could not understand it.

"So it was deliberate," said Sadie.

"Could hardly be an accident now, could it?" Kevin was tight-lipped. He straightened himself, gazed out across to the hills, as if for inspiration. He sighed. "I'm sorry, Jack."

"I don't know what to do."

"The police?" said Sadie.

"I can't go to the police now, can I? Report my wife for running off."

His wife. Was she really that? They had been married but a few hours before, and yet here he was legally responsible for her.

"She really is a little—" Sadie stopped. What use was there in finishing the sentence? She looked at Kevin. Jack was looking at him too, waiting to be told what to do.

"I'm afraid you'll have to go to the police, Jack. She's on probation. You're her next of kin. But wait till tomorrow. You never know . . ."

Jack drove off.

"Poor soul," said Sadie. "Do you think Clodagh will come back?"

"No, I don't. But I didn't think he was in any fit state to go to the police today."

"He's had enough for one day, I should think. Married and left before nightfall, God help him!"

Kevin's face, which at the cottage had been light, was dark again. Sadie raged at Clodagh, calling her names, wishing her at the bottom of the Irish Sea.

"She's the most selfish creature I've ever clapped eyes on!"

"I know, I know." He sighed. "But she is my sister."

"More's the pity! I hope she stays out of our road at any rate."

"I expect she will. I don't think she wants to be a nuisance to us."

"Just to everyone else."

"She's her own worst enemy," said Kevin quietly. "But how can you make anyone see that?"

They drove the rest of the way up to the house in silence and Sadie took Brendan off for tea and bed. She scrambled egg vigorously, cursing Clodagh, slopping egg on the cooker. Damn the girl! Why did she have to spoil their afternoon at the cottage?

"Your aunt is a pain in the neck, Brendan, along with a few other McCoys whose names I might mention!"

But by the time she was putting the boy into his cot she had calmed. She told him a bed-time story about a cottage in a field full of snowdrops.

"You'll just love it, boyo." She tucked him in firmly. "Won't you now?"

"No," he declared, making her laugh and at the same time bringing a catch to her throat.

Outside, Kevin was raking the gravel at the top of the drive, making use of the last shreds of daylight. The witching hour, some folks called it. He loved this time of day much more than bright noon, even though there was often an edge of sadness to it. As there was today. He was thinking of his sister of whom he had grown fond and about whom he was concerned, but who seemed to have embarked on a course of self-destruction. He felt helpless to help her. Perhaps he would just have to accept that it was beyond him.

He leant on the rake to watch the sun go down. Suddenly he frowned, straightened. A car had turned in at the end of the drive.

"What is it, Kev?" asked Sadie, who had just come out of the house.

"There's a car coming."

"Not Jack again?"

With Clodagh perhaps? But, no, it was not Jack's car; this one was light coloured, and very small.

"Someone you know?"

"I think—"

"Well?"

"I'm almost sure—"

"Who in the name of goodness is it then? Would you be for telling me?"

The car was coming steadily closer.

"It looks a bit like one of those invalid cars," said Sadie.

"It is," said Kevin. "Indeed I believe, Sadie—yes, I do—Uncle Albert's come to visit us!"